AFRICAN WRITERS SERIES

*Editorial Adviser · Chinua Achebe*

40

# A Woman in her Prime

# AFRICAN WRITERS SERIES

Asare Konadu

# *A Woman in her Prime*

**HEINEMANN**
LONDON   IBADAN   NAIROBI

Heinemann Educational Books Ltd
48 Charles Street, London W1X 8AH
PMB 5205, Ibadan · POB 25080, Nairobi

EDINBURGH   MELBOURNE   TORONTO
AUCKLAND   SINGAPORE   HONG KONG


SBN 435 90040 4


© Asare Konadu 1967
First published by William Heinemann 1967
First published in African Writers Series 1967
Reprinted 1969.

Printed in Malta by
St Paul's Press Ltd

## *Note*

For a glossary of Ghanaian words
and phrases, see page 108.

# Chapter One

TODAY was Friday and the day of sacrifice for the great god Tano.

Pokuwaa returned home from her last trip to the river and went quickly into the kitchen to place the water there ready for use. Daybreak was near and her excitement was mounting. She ran through the compound to the bathroom outside her hut, bumping into the bamboo enclosure in her haste. She stripped off her clothes and scooped the water over her body. The water was a bit chilly in the morning air. She should have heated it, she thought, 'but if it saves me a little bit of time . . .' Time at Brenhoma was counted by the sun and now although the sun was still behind the clouds, very soon it would break out and the shadows could lengthen. Speeding up, she slipped on the stone floor and had to step into the wooden water container to steady herself.

Very soon the house of Tano would begin to fill with people, and she had to hurry to get there in time for her turn at consultation and sacrifice. She could feel inside her the drums that would sound for the gathering for sacrifice in all the neighbourhood. People would bring yams, sheep, goats, eggs, cowries. What a person had to sacrifice depended on

1

her requirements. In some cases people were asked to bring cows.

Pokuwaa thought how lucky it was for her that it had to be simply a hen and eggs; though it had been difficult getting a hen that was black all over.

She dashed back to her room, rubbed her limbs with some shea cream; then she sprayed herself with smooth white clay powder. This was for purification and it was essential on this day of sacrifice. That done, she hurried out of her room with her calabash full of eggs.

Where was the black hen? Pokuwaa went to the post where the hen had been tied and at sight of the broken string, her mouth fell open. She began to tremble. Who could have given that string a twist and broken it? She rushed outside and began searching under the small bushes there.

'What evil spirit wants to spoil the day for me?' she moaned. 'Help me, O Almighty. Help me.'

She ran into her room to get some more grain. With this she started off to look for the hen in the village. If she could see it, she would spread the corn to lure it back to her.

For three days she had kept watch over the black hen and today, the day of the sacrifice, the hen was missing. It had been difficult to obtain such a hen in the vicinity of her own village, Brenhoma, and she had had to travel over six miles to buy one from the next village, Nsutem. The owner had insisted on taking two hundred cowries for it. Pokuwaa had tried to bargain for one hundred and sixty, and the owner, who knew the value of that black hen, had refused. These jet-black hens were always being sought after, and if this buyer didn't buy it, another was bound to come along some day. Someone else would be quite willing to pay two hundred cowries.

So Pokuwaa had paid and taken the hen to Brenhoma, put a single bead on its leg for identification and tied it up for safety. And now the hen was gone.

'But it was there this morning,' she remembered. 'I spread some corn for it.' She looked round again.

'"Eat well, this might be your last feed," I said as I spread the corn. And it pecked eagerly and swallowed the lot before I could leave the house to collect another pot of water from the river. I went into the room with the water-pots, picked up the last pot and came out to find that it had already finished all the corn. I said, "You need more. You must eat to keep alive. I need your blood." I put down my pot, went back inside, scooped another handful of grain and spread it for the hen before I left the house.'

Further than this she could not remember. Had the hen been there when she returned from the half-mile walk to the river? She couldn't remember. On her way down to the river she had been busy with her prayerful thoughts, beseeching her ancestors and the gods to bless her efforts to get a child. She had prayed to God:

> 'You are not an unforgiving God,
> God of our forefathers.
> Your assistance is not temporary.
> You are almighty.
> Let all evil men fall before you.'

3

The importance of this Fofie, this festive Friday which came once every six weeks, had crowded her mind. This day, gods and goddesses moved among men to feast and grant people's requests. And they were powerful. They could answer her need for a child. The ancestors of her father and mother would surely help her. If she herself had wronged anyone or if the sins of her parents or ancestors were being avenged on her, the deities could be besought to spare her the pain of not having a child of her own. That was why she had been told to get the black hen. Jet black, that was it. Was the black hen not there when she returned from this last trip to the river?

What had happened in fact was quite simple: as soon as Pokuwaa had gone out of the house a cock had come along and joined in the feast. Then he had started making approaches to the hen. It was not easy in the game with a string round the hen's legs and so in the struggle that followed the string made of old raffia palm had snapped. The hen, now freed, had followed the cock out of the shed, and out of the yard. The hen had taken a dust bath, and then the two of them had ventured out into a narrow lane leading to the bush outside the village.


Pokuwaa rushed along at first, but, seeing no sign of the black hen, she slowed down in an attempt to look more closely in nooks and corners among the crowding huts.

Soon she came upon some children playing in a lane. 'Children,' she pleaded, 'have you seen a black hen here?' One of them started to run away. 'Why,' she called, 'come back! I want you to help me find my black hen.'

4

One of the children soon volunteered an explanation. 'He is running away because he has been throwing stones at a black hen which passed . . . '

'What?' interrupted Pokuwaa eagerly,

'. . . at a black hen which passed here a few minutes ago. That is why he is running away,' he continued.

'Show me where you saw the hen,' said Pokuwaa, controlling herself.

'There!' many eager mouths shouted; and many hands pointed towards the bush outside the village.

'Where? Come with me and show me.' Pokuwaa now addressed herself to the little boy who was said to have been throwing stones at the hen. He looked younger than his seven years, and had bushy hair with cowries and shells tied in it.

Pokuwaa looked at this boy and felt immediate sympathy for him. She knew that such children should not be harshly treated, let alone beaten. For it was feared that if they were beaten the fetish would take them away. And so they were pampered and especially cared for.

'Take me where you threw stones at the hen,' entreated Pokuwaa, reaching for the hand of the fetish child.

The other children trooped after them. Soon they reached a mango tree.

'That was where I first saw the hen. It was with a group of fowls, but it cackled the loudest, and I threw a branch. I just threw a branch,' he rattled on. 'And it went over there.'

Pokuwaa was now getting impatient. She looked at the rising sun in the crimson sky, and knew that if she was to get to Tano's home in time, she would have to hurry. It was with

5

an effort that she reminded herself that she mustn't get cross with a fetish child. It was one such child that she herself was seeking—and if she was successful . . .

'Oh, God,' she groaned, 'who could have set that hen free? Who?'

They were almost at the bush outside the village, and there was nothing to do but to enter it and search there also. By now she was really worried.

Could this perhaps be the work of evil spirits who, knowing Tano's greatness, had spirited the hen away, to stop her from making her sacrifice? She knew, at least she had been told, of ghosts who walked the streets at night, of fiery witches who stayed on tree-tops doing all kinds of wickedness. They had power to turn things into small objects and, through incantations, spirit them away. She had been told of a child who had been turned into a chicken and slaughtered; of a man who had turned himself into a croco-dile and devoured a young girl who had jilted him.

'But here I am,' Pokuwaa thought aloud, 'taking the words of Tano seriously. And now I can't find the black hen.' It had been on a Friday six weeks ago that, in the unlit room of Tano's shrine, the oracles had told her to bring this black hen and eggs to be offered to the spirits so that they might bring her madwowa back to her. She had sacrificed four times before; white cloth, and cowries in tens, without any success; but this time the demand for sacrifice had come from Tano himself, and Tano was great.

'Great Tano,' she cried, 'assist me in my plight. You are powerful and nobody can thwart your will.'

Would she find this hen in time, or was this day to

6

be lost to her even if she did find it—if she found it too late?

'What a world. When you find the hoe you can't find the stick. When you find the stick you can't find the hoe. Oh, Adwoa Pokuwaa! I am in a tight lane.' She was weeping now, seized with the fear that if she failed to make the sacrifice and lost this chance of bearing a child, her fate as a barren woman would be made certain. Then her old age would be doomed to loneliness; no child to care for her, no grandchild to warm her compound and no issue of her blood at all to mourn at her death. She would be buried of course by the relatives and her brothers' children would be there, but there was nothing better than having your own children at your funeral.

The children with her had turned the search into a game of hide-and-seek. Some went behind bushes, throwing pebbles at each other and imitating bird and animal sounds. Others were giving chase. Only the fetish child continued to search with Pokuwaa.

They were getting into denser bush when her eyes fell on a shiny black back, through a tangle of thorny stems. Her heart leaped and she thrust her arm through the thorns without caution. Her hand was stabbed, but as she withdrew it what she noticed more than the pain was the blood that dripped on to the green leaves at her feet. She was fascinated by the red of her blood, and a thought ran through her that with this red fire in her, this fine blood, she was certainly young enough to have a child.

Why was the hen so still? Was it dead? The noise from the children should be enough to startle it if it was not dead.

And yet dead hens always lay on their back or on their side, never on their belly. If this turned out to be a hen indeed, and alive, and with a single bead on its foot, then her day was saved.

She broke off a branch and began to push the thorns aside to make an opening, and before she knew it the fetish child had shot through to the other side and was making his way towards that black back in the bushes beyond. There could be no mistaking that cackling. It was a hen. But why was the fetish child pulling? They both saw why at once. They saw the black snake that had been trying to swallow the hen. Then everything happened at once. The fetish child shot back in fear; the children screamed and ran away; and Pokuwaa tore her way through the thorns towards the black hen and the black snake. She wasn't afraid of snakes. She had killed one at an early age and had lost her fear of them long since. Soon the black snake was flattened out on the ground and she was pinning it down with the sharp end of the branch in order to pull out the leg of the hen, which had been swallowed up to the thigh, while the hen flapped and cackled hysterically.

Pokuwaa was aware of a sense of triumph. If the black snake was a bad spirit, or a man turned into a snake, it had been conquered.

The first round of her battle was over. A prayer was on her lips as she ran the whole way home:

'Okatakyi Brempong,
Leader of men, linguist of all gods.
You know the deep and see what comes.

The rest of the fight is in your hand.
Okatakyi, my praises of you will never end.'

When she arrived breathless in her compound, Kwadwo Fordwuo was standing there, waiting.

'Come,' she panted, 'I'll tell you about all this when we're on our way. We are lucky to be getting there at all. I'll fetch my eggs.'

# Chapter Two

THE god Tano was carried on the head of a middle-aged man strongly built in the shoulders. He was in a state of possession. With him in the room was the priest.

'Rub the leaves in your left hand, and as the juice emerges, rub it on your body. After your bath with the water boiled with the tree barks, drink a cupful of the bath brew, and walk quickly to the house without turning back. All this should be done very early in the morning just as the dawn breaks.' The priest issuing these instructions after the consultation held his own ears by way of emphasising to Pokuwaa the importance of her listening with care. Kwadwo had come into the room also after the consultation was over, and he was standing beside Pokuwaa, nodding heavily as if the instructions were as much for him.

When it was all over, they bowed and left the shrine. Outside, other people were waiting their turns at consultation and sacrifice.

'I'm going to spend this whole week with you while you perform these purification rites,' Kwadwo was saying. His voice was comforting.

Pokuwaa, who hadn't expected him to offer to do this for

her, was pleased; yet, wanting to test him, she asked, 'What about your wife?'

She knew that Kwadwo's wife had the right to resent such an arrangement, but in her heart she hoped that he meant it.

'What about your wife?' she insisted softly. 'She won't like it.' She looked straight at Kwadwo for his response. 'You'd better go back to her,' she said, turning her eyes away.

'No. She will understand,' said Kwadwo slowly. 'I shall explain your problem to her.'

They walked on in silence to Pokuwaa's house.

That night, when Kwadwo returned to her, she asked him whether his wife agreed to the arrangement.

'She says she does not mind,' he calmly replied. 'Her only prayer is that this does help you to get a child.'

He knew he was lying. The talk with his wife had only resulted in a quarrel. She had protested vehemently against his spending all that week with Pokuwaa, saying that she would not sell her rights to any barren woman. Kwadwo had left the house in anger. Even as he told his lie now, he was looking for shadows, fearing that his angry wife might rush in at any minute to make trouble.

That night seemed to last a long time. Pokuwaa talked to Kwadwo endlessly to keep sleep away. 'I don't feel any of the excitement I used to feel on previous occasions when I had to make a sacrifice,' she said.

'Perhaps,' Kwadwo suggested, 'that is a sign of greater confidence in success. Let's hope that a child will come this time.'

'Do you believe that? I am looking forward to that day.' Pokuwaa's voice was sad. 'Oh, how I shall cling to that child . . . even if I have to stay away from work on the farm,' she sighed.

Kwadwo laughed. 'And what will you eat?' he asked gently.

'God is there. We shall eat,' Pokuwaa replied, sighing again.

'Yes,' said Kwadwo. 'He will give us to eat . . . if we work.'

Pokuwaa laughed in the darkness, and added, 'I remember the story of the two men who went to the Denteh fetish for consultations. One was told he would become rich and prosperous; the other that he would die in poverty.'

'Yes, I know,' Kwadwo interrupted. The story was a well-known joke. 'And the one who had been promised wealth sat under the village silk cotton tree waiting for his fortune, while the other man applied himself on his farm.'

'And who was it who died in poverty?' asked Pokuwaa.

'Are you asking me?' laughed Kwadwo. They were both laughing as they recited together, 'The one who was waiting for the gods to provide.'

Pokuwaa stretched her limbs in the bed murmuring, 'Yes, it does seem that, in this world of ours, those promised impending riches never get them.'

Kwadwo was tired. He hadn't slept for two nights. He had been attending a funeral celebration at Ninting. It was not a small effort to return from there in time for Pokuwaa's consultation at Tanofie. Ninting was a long journey from Brenhoma.

'If you hadn't been worried about the black hen this morning,' he said, turning to her, 'you would have had to worry about my not arriving here at the time you expected me. Part of the distance I had to run. You would have laughed to see me jumping over logs, and rushing as if someone was pursuing me.' He touched her as she laughed tenderly in the dark. 'And all that rushing was on a stomach that had been punished with funeral fasting for two days. I wish we didn't have to wait for the dead to be buried before we can eat.'

'Don't tell me you mind fasting at your own grandfather's funeral.' Pokuwaa knew Kwadwo wouldn't take offence at this. 'Besides,' she teased, 'what about all the palm wine you men take the opportunity to drink just because custom allows you to kill your thirst?'

'If you women envy us that, let me testify to you that pots of palm wine on an empty belly do the body no good at all.'

'Then why . . .?'

'Pokuwaa!' Kwadwo didn't have to say any more than that to stop her pursuing the subject. They both laughed again.

'Soon after the old man was quietly in his pit, and the last of my responsibilities had been carried out, I left Ninting with some other people. I was in so great a hurry that I got far ahead of them.' Kwadwo smiled to himself as he heard again in his head the sound of his own mellow voice shouting to his fellow travellers to speed up, and echoing through the forest strangely in the darkness before dawn.

'Also,' he continued, 'I prayed.'

The room became very quiet as he sat thinking of how he

had prayed as his feet brushed the dew. He had called on great Tano to make it possible for Pokuwaa to bear a child. The thought that she had divorced two earlier husbands because she couldn't have a child with them had come strongly to him then, and he had vowed to do everything he could to help make the sacrifices a success. He was very anxious to save his own marriage with this woman.

These heavy thoughts were a burden. He fell back, pulled the cotton blanket over his head, and went to sleep. Pokuwaa whispered, 'Are you asleep?' and as there was no answer, she busied herself for a little while with the lamp. The rag wick in the earthen pot was sputtering and would soon go out. She always had a supply of good oil skimmed from palm soup. With some of this she filled the lamp. It was soon burning steadily again. As she slipped quietly beside Kwadwo again he felt her touch and stirred.

'You must not leave me to sleep alone,' she murmured. 'Sometimes when I'm alone like that I begin to wish I had a husband of my own.'

'You mean, I am not the man for you?' he asked.

'I mean someone who hasn't got another wife. And then I shall not have lonely nights, and can come close to him when I hear ghosts moving through the night, and fear.'

Kwadwo touched her and said, 'Pokuwaa.' And she could feel that he was there. Did this feeling of wanting him always by her side mean that she loved him? She knew that whenever he wasn't with her she felt dejected and insecure. And then she would lie in bed turning all night till cockcrow when signs of day would bring relief. She would get up then and pick up her pot to fetch water. She would anxiously count the three days he had to spend away with his other wife.

'Yes,' she thought, 'without a child I am a person who needs your company. When you're away, I'm alone. But, if the high God is there, who comforts people, some day I shall have my own child to comfort and keep me company. A matter of time . . . and luck. Oh, Adwoa! What luck is mine! People get children without going through half the troubled oath I'm travelling now. I can't sleep, and I am always waiting for the dawn.'

She sat up and watched Kwadwo's calm, sleeping face. She drew nearer to him and lying down pulled part of the blanket over herself. Sharing in his calmness, she herself was soon visited by sleep.

Kwadwo was first to wake up. He found Pokuwaa still by his side, and realised that the white clay marks were not on her body. The scent of pepre seeds with which she should besmear herself was also absent. And it was already daylight. His heart gave a big thump. He lifted her bodily and sat her up. The sun was already shining. He could hear birds, and the fowls and goats outside.

Pokuwaa rubbed her eyes, looked round, and becoming aware of the situation, cried with despair, 'Alas! The first day of sacrifice is lost.'

# Chapter Three

'AKYE O, Pokuwaa!' Pokuwaa didn't have to go out into the compound to see who had come to see her. Only Koramoa said good morning like that. And how welcome she was on this day.

'I'm coming,' she called, relieved to have a friend to help her to forget the gloomy thoughts with which she had been sitting inside her room since Kwadwo had left. She had had an ordinary bath, and could not find any spirit in her to do her household duties. She had even started to have some doubts. She observed that the list of barks and herbs given her at Tanofie was the same as had been given her the previous year by a herbalist at Mmuoho. She went over the list again and asked herself, 'Why then didn't I bear a child at that time?' Since then she had carried out other sacrifices; giving away cowries to the destitute, sacrificing, on two occasions, a cock to her father's spirit. She had done all this with the readiness that a new wife applies to her duties.

'Akye o, Koramoa.' Her eyes fell on the child her friend was carrying in her arms.

'Yaa Peafo,' Koramoa responded. She knew and enjoyed using formal appellations like that. 'I saw you as you walked out of Tano's house yesterday, but you didn't even greet me.'

Pokuwaa sighed, 'Hm.' She remembered seeing Koramoa and her husband waiting outside.

'We were going to do our thanksgiving sacrifice,' Koramoa informed her.

There was no point in Pokuwaa asking what for. She knew it was thanksgiving to Tano for helping them to have a child. She had watched the whole course of events. Koramoa was full of praise for Tano when she was expecting the child. Every Fofie she danced at the drumming. She gave birth without any mishap.

'How is life this morning?' asked Koramoa. She hitched the child to her side, wrapped part of her cloth round him, and placed her breast in his little mouth.

The two friends sat down and talked about their farms at Bentenkoro, but most of the time Pokuwaa's eyes rested on the child, and in her mind's eye she pictured the day when she would be holding her own in her arms.

'How old is the baby now?' she asked after a while, reaching playfully for the child's hand.

'About five months. I shall never forget the trouble he gave me while in my womb. And now he is born, he is always crying. I never have time to myself,' Koramoa proudly complained.

'He will soon grow and you will be free,' was all Pokuwaa could make herself remark.

'When will that happen?' her friend went on. 'That will be years from now.'

Pokuwaa smiled kindly. 'It will come one day,' she said.

17

'One day,' Koramoa rejoined. 'It is indeed true that man is never without any trouble on his head. Now, I wish somebody would take care of him to make me free again.'

'You mean you are wishing for the days of our girlhood when we were gay and playful?'

The question brought happy laughter from Koramoa. 'Oh, we shall never have those days again,' she declared. 'Girls of these times have nothing of the time we had.'

She and Pokuwaa had been playmates in their girlhood. Not much had happened or changed since then at Brenhoma. Just as they had done, girls still played Ampe, and also Asɔgoro in which they lined up to sing songs of praise and admonition, in solo and chorus, and also in song made references to their boy friends. Pokuwaa remembered that she had found it very thrilling at the age of five to learn to count in the Ampe jumping game. Koramoa agreed with her that the Ampe game was every little girl's favourite. 'But,' she reminded her friend, 'think of all that came out of Asɔgoro!'

'I am sure,' Pokuwaa said, 'that Kofi Dede, your husband, has forgotten by now that it was through our Asɔgoro that the two of you developed your love affair.'

'And I am sure,' Koramoa replied, 'that wherever Kofi Daafo may be, he will always remember those days.'

Kofi Daafo was Pokuwaa's first husband. She and Koramoa had met these husbands at the same time, and from the playground had carried their childlike affairs into serious reality and married. Koramoa stuck to her husband, and for years people thought she was not going to bear a

18

child. Pokuwaa remembered that when she divorced Kofi Daafo, her friend was also tempted to think of a break for the same reason.

'Now you see,' she said aloud, 'if you had divorced Kofi Dede, you would perhaps be as I am today.'

'Why? Is he the only fruitful man in the world?'

Pokuwaa knew that Koramoa didn't mean this remark to be taken seriously, so she said, 'You cannot deny that this child has blessed a long union. What I'm trying to tell you is that I might have profited in the same way if I had stayed in one place like you.'

Koramoa had to leave, and as she hitched the child on to her back and tied her cloth firmly round him, she still complained that there might be good reason in what Pokuwaa said, but 'the child is giving me too much trouble already, and I'm beginning to doubt if he will give me the happiness I dreamed of.'

After saying goodbye outside, Pokuwaa returned to her house thinking how true it was that memories could not be brought back to life. When she sat down, thoughts of Kwaku Fosu, her second husband, came to her mind. She had been fond of that man, but there was no child, and she divorced him. Her mother used to come and say, 'You see, my child, you should have children. You are my only daughter, and unless you have a child our lives will end miserably.'

'But mother, what can I do?'

'You have been married to Kwaku Fosu for nearly three years. There is no sign of a child. Will you still stick to him?'

'But mother, we cannot force a child. We'll leave it to

19

God. Besides it is not easy to walk up to a man and tell him, "I have divorced you; go!" I can only do that if he actually does me wrong.'

After this from time to time her mother brought little faults to her notice. 'The other day,' she reminded her, 'he didn't come with you to the farm even though he knew well you needed him.'

But it was something quite trivial that Pokuwaa eventually took up with Kwaku Fosu and broke the marriage.

Then she met Kwadwo Fordwuo. In the very first month of their meeting Pokuwaa's blood failed to appear. Then there were signs in her breasts. O God! There were signs that she was expecting a baby. One month passed. She told her mother.

'Keep quiet about it,' the happy woman counselled her daughter. 'Don't tell anybody.'

Pokuwaa's excitement grew. But one morning she saw her blood again. It was a drop, then a streak, and then a flow.

'Mother, I am seeing blood again.'

'Let me see,' she said, afraid to believe it. It was blood. She took Pokuwaa to the medicine man.

'Your child is having a miscarriage because you never sent sacrifices in thanksgiving to the fetish which gave her to you. You remember Anowuo?'

Pokuwaa's mother nodded, but desperately implored, 'Can't you do something for us?'

'No,' answered the man. 'This conception will be lost, but if you carry out the sacrifice, another child will come very soon.'

'What is required for the sacrifice?'

'I can see the fetish in here,' said the man after his incantations. 'It demands a white sheep, eggs, and a length of white cloth.'

The mother paid three cowries for the consultation.

That was Pokuwaa's first and only experience of childbearing. She cried a lot, but she took the event as proof that if she continued with Kwadwo, another child would come.

He had another wife who already had two children by him at the time Pokuwaa met him. Another was born to them soon after this miscarriage. Pokuwaa's friends knew how depressed she was with her misfortune and they came in to comfort her, sitting round and doing jobs in the house.

'Do not weep so much over it,' they said. 'If you do, your ɔkra will be saddened, and will turn its back on you. If you weep things will not happen as destined for you,' they explained.

'But things are already not happening right for me. Adwoa, what luck I have. Me nkrabea nye.'

Her friends felt her sorrow and wiped the tears from her face.

'I do not know what I have done to the gods,' she moaned. 'The very thing for which I have sacrificed often, passes away.'

She could not accept comfort even from Kwadwo himself, who tried to keep her mind on the possibility of another chance. For some time, she could not bear it when he talked of this probability, and for many days she spread a grass mat on the other side of the hut to sleep by herself.

'These thoughts,' she sighed. 'Why do they come to press on my soul?' She got up from the yard determined to forget

21

—and yet when she reached her room, she knew she didn't have the spirit for doing anything else. She spread her mat to lie on it and think.

The days of her early youth were with her. She was one of the girls whose hand had been asked for before coming of age.

When they became engaged all the girls liked to display their wrists on which their engagement bracelets were tied. And in fact the red parrot feather and rich yellow beads did look attractive on their soft wrists. A girl would go to all sorts of tricks to get someone to notice her bracelet and ask, 'Oh, has your fiance tied his Akyikyibaso on your arm?'

Pokuwaa was beautiful, plump and deep dark. When they tied her Akyikyibaso on her wrist to engage her to her young fiancé Kofi Daafo, people said they had never seen a sight so enchanting before.

'And then the days came when mother said I couldn't go out,' she said aloud. That time was so puzzling, so strange and so full of joy. She couldn't go anywhere during her seven days' ceremony. She was forbidden to do anything besides eating and sleeping. 'Yes, some memories are good after all.' She could feel a little comfort in thinking of how attentive her mother had been to the correctness of her outdooring ceremony.

'You are my only daughter. My five sons will have children for their wives' families; but the child that you will bear will be my own grandchild,' her mother had explained. She had praised the gods that her Pokuwaa was already engaged. Some girls, she said, had been known to sit for months and even years after their outdooring before getting a child.

Pokuwaa became quite cheered, thinking of her outdooring. She could see clearly the scene in the village meeting ground when she was openly declared to have come of age. The drums thrilled her. The women who had come for her sake to share her ceremony, danced the length of the main street and back to where she sat under the silk cotton tree on her high stool among her ceremonial maids and other girls, and surrounded by the presents from the man who was already acknowledged her husband. Her foot was on her future path, and she and everybody else there knew that her next step would be to give birth to a child. She knew that Kofi Daafo was proud of her. They played like friends and often talked about how they would treat their child when it was born.

She knew he loved her. He had a habit of turning playfully and whispering something in her ear. She wouldn't hear, but she knew he was telling her something about his love. When he was not with her he was at his father's house. They went to work on the farm together. People said that she was using charms on him, but Kofi knew better. In her company he always radiated happiness, and she knew this meant he was happy with her.

Then the first year, and the second year passed. There was no child. She remembered that this had made her heart afraid because of the people of Brenhoma. To them, to be barren was the worst that could happen to a woman. The approach of her time caused her apprehension every month. Seeing her blood saddened her deeply. She had a talk with her mother.

'And that is when the story of my sacrifices began,' Pokuwaa said aloud, turning over to press her face into her pillow.

'Who is that?' she called, for she had heard somebody in the yard.

She heard a child's voice saying, 'Me.' Pokuwaa jumped up and ran out. She saw standing there with shining eyes the tiny daughter of Afua Fofie, her neighbour.

There was something between Pokuwaa and children. They would always come to her. But whatever she did for them their mothers always came and took them away. She lifted up the child and took her into her kitchen to give her food. They were sitting there talking like friends when Afua Fofie entered the yard, looking for her child. There she sat eating. Without even a greeting, Afua Fofie reached for the child and gave her a slap on her face.

'Why, Afua?' asked Pokuwaa, feeling very hurt. Instead of replying to the question, Afua addressed the child. 'I have told you not to come here again,' she shouted.

'Why?' Pokuwaa asked again.

'Listen, I am not talking to you,' said Afua, dragging the child along.

Pokuwaa was very angry at this but the child was not her child.

'Don't ever think I shall ever do harm to your child. May God forbid,' she said, almost crying.

'The child is my child. I have every right to take her away, without explaining myself to you,' said Afua rudely, as she left the yard.

'Kra Adwoa,' said Pokuwaa, 'don't get sad. This will not

24

go on for ever. Some day we also shall have cause to be glad.'

She rose from the kitchen and walked to the gate. Standing there, she could hear children's voices in the town. How many of them had called her mother when she played with them. And even when she was a young girl herself and she and her friends played mothers and children, they all wanted her to be mother because she was soft and mature-looking.

At times there were more than one mother, but the children would rally to her side and climb on her thighs and make believe with 'Mother, mother, mother.' She liked the very sound, and she acted like her own mother, saying, 'Oh, don't worry me, children. Why are you always so troublesome?'

They would fall off, and come again. She would put one across her lap and smack her bottom. But however playfully she tried to be hard, she was always the centre of their attraction, and they came. 'And even if those days were spent in dreams, why have the children I loved so well deserted me?'

She walked out of her house towards Afua Fofie's house to see if the child was still being beaten. Hearing no sound, she was returning home when two other little girls saw her and ran to her.

She was glad, but she said to them, 'You'd better go to your mothers. They might be looking for you.'

'No, we will stay. It is not dark yet,' the older one said pleadingly.

'No, you can come another time.' She took their hands, walked them a little way, and went back to her kitchen.

In a few minutes she saw a head peeping through the

kitchen window. When she walked towards the gate the two children she had sent away started running away. 'Ama Foriwa, wait for me, don't leave me behind.'

Pokuwaa smiled. 'Children will be children, never thinking of anything but their play.'

She entered her room. 'I should stick to Kwadwo, and leave the rest to God,' she thought. 'Even if it breaks my heart to do it, it is best to attempt to build new memories.'

# Chapter Four

As she concluded the rites of her purification, Pokuwaa became more optimistic. Each morning, on rising, she went to the outskirts of the village and, standing over a log of the onwoma tree, she scooped water, in which the herbs had been boiled, over her body seven times.

The planting season had started. She worked lightly on the farms and didn't carry any heavy loads. Her mother insisted on this, doing most of the housework for her.

'You must not work hard,' she counselled. 'You must conserve your strength for the child.'

Pokuwaa tried to tell her that she felt quite strong and that working was better than sitting idly around.

'You do not know how tiring it is to bear a child,' the mother countered. 'You will live to remember the experience. When you were being expected the headaches and the fevers I had! Most of the time. But your father was very sympathetic and did many things for me. Things are not what they used to be. The men of today don't care as much about their wives. Indeed times have changed.'

When six months passed without result Pokuwaa wondered whether purification and sacrifices would ever cease to be part of her life. She had been told at Tanofie that if she did the things requested of her she would not have to wait for more than three months for a child. True that she had lost a day of the rites, but she had gone through the remaining days punctually and correctly. Keeping watch and seeing nothing happening, she went to see Tano again.

'There is no result yet,' she told the priest. 'But Tano is a great god who can correct anything that is going wrong.'

She knelt down for the priest to hold above her head the white tail of a horse—or was it a cow? He lifted it three times and she felt fine particles of sand falling out of the tail onto her shoulders. She dared not look up to see as that would mean challenging the god. So she kept her position, her head bent down.

'Tell me how you went through the ceremony. The oracles say you did not do as commanded,' the priest said.

'I am here to find out what went wrong, nana,' said Pokuwaa submissively.

'Tell me how you went through the rites,' the priest said again. 'You did something wrong.'

Pokuwaa narrated her story, adding, 'You said I should not look back as I walked home.'

'Yes, that is where you went wrong. It was not once, but twice that you looked back.'

That was correct. Pokuwaa's knees trembled. On the first occasion she had left her sponge behind and turned back for it. On the second, she thought she heard footsteps and turned to see who it was. When she did, she saw a man crossing from one side of the path to the other and wondered what he was doing there at that time. She ran home, scared that she had seen a ghost. 'How do these fetishes see everything?' she thought as she knelt there.

The priest said, 'Now, my child, go back home and do as you are told. You will be given another collection of the herbs. Boil them in water and use the water to bathe for seven days, and then come and see me.'

She bowed and withdrew from the presence of the priest. His linguist whisked her away and gave her the herbs prescribed.

If her only mistake last time was that she looked back, she was determined that nothing of the kind should happen again. At home, Kwadwo asked her to repeat the drill again in his hearing.

He was now really apprehensive about Pokuwaa's barrenness, fearing that with the years passing away she would wake up one day and demand divorce. It had happened to her two earlier husbands, and he never ruled out the possibility. Whatever he did he bore at the back of his mind that he had a superior duty to Pokuwaa and that was to see that she had her own child. As she went over the things she had been instructed to do, he listened with concentration, in order to help her not to forget anything.

Pokuwaa boiled the herbs overnight in a pot of fresh water from the river. At the first peep of dawn, for seven days, she got up, poured some of the herbal water into a small pot and walked to the outskirts of the village. There, standing over the same log of the onwoma tree, she scooped the water over her body seven times, repeating words of incantation. She concentrated hardest on walking straight home without looking back. Arriving home she dabbed herself

29

with pepre and white clay, filling the room with a mixed scent of tree barks and clover. If Kwadwo was asleep she nudged him. He woke up and sniffed the scent of the pepre. 'That is nice,' he said. 'You'd better get nearer.' He held her close and rubbed his nose into her neck where the scent was strongest.

They took delight in each other, and Pokuwaa was conscious that during this time she was hanging on Kwadwo's praises and admiration. She dressed in new clothes and paraded for him to see her and say she was nice. It wasn't Kwadwo's normal way to speak his praises. Once when he said he didn't like the clothes she wore, Pokuwaa broke out crying. He learned his lesson. Also, he did enjoy the way his admiration sent her walking with her chest out and swinging her arms luxuriantly.

The rains had begun. The two of them worked hopefully together. She made yam mounds, prepared the seed yams, dug her fingers into the raised earth and planted, enjoying it like a child, but working hard. She promised herself that she would teach her child this work. Many times, she returned home quite late.

Kwadwo often went with her to the farm, carrying his cutlass and walking ahead. He made jokes as he cut through the climbers that nosed their way into the footpath to clear the way.

They worried about the heaviness of the rains and the rats that were eating their way through the farms; especially as these animals were uprooting the yams germinating in the mounds.

Kwadwo made adwaa round Pokuwaa's farm to protect,

30

it. It took quite a long time to cut palm branches and stake them in, but the adwaa proved effective in barring off the rats.

'People of Brenhoma are lazy,' Kwadwo complained. 'It will not take the people of another place a week's hunting to kill the rats that trouble them. Here, they sit and watch them running through their huts.'

'Don't put so much salt into it,' said Pokuwaa, 'although you are right to say they ought to do something. Why not suggest a hunting to the community?'

'Who am I?' said Kwadwo. 'The elders should take the initiative if they are worthy of being the leaders of men. The other night, as I walked behind Opanin Kofi Mensah in the dark, I coughed and he started running. How can such an elder make serious decisions?'

'Wait,' Pokuwaa warned, 'it will be your turn to become an elder very soon.'

'Yes, and then we shall take a man's decision to fight the animals, not walk with women to collect snails.'

Kwadwo had a gun that his father had given him. Sometimes it failed to fire, and during the dry season he had spent time mending and cleaning it. He took it regularly to the farm and succeeded once in a while in shooting a deer or antelope. He also spent time between the planting and the harvest weaving new mats for Pokuwaa's door.

For friendship, he sat sometimes with other men under the silk cotton tree to drink palm wine from a special calabash which he took pride in cleaning himself. Pokuwaa, not wanting him to drink, hid the calabash many times saying, 'Wine is not food, and should not be taken in excess.'

31

He was a man and a man must drink, was Kwadwo's retort. When she asked him what he gained out of it he declared, 'Power. Full power,' not sounding at all like the man round whom the earth had moved at his first calabash of palm wine.

'Left alone I know you will not drink,' tried Pokuwaa again. 'It is Kofi Badu who is drawing you into bad company.'

Kwadwo swore that on the contrary his friend Kofi Badu was a very good man. 'I dread what I would be without his counsel.'

'Counsel about wine?' asked Pokuwaa, meaning to be saucy.

Happily for her there was plenty of work on the farm for them. Sometimes she tired and was conscious of ageing, but these were things she didn't like to think about. Her mother was helping her with housework, it was true—but supposing she couldn't fetch water? Staring her in the face were sure indications of a lonely old age.

One Saturday, as she was hurrying to her farm, another woman joined her at the outskirts of the village. They had a mile to walk before branching off to their different farms, and the company was welcome to both. Their pace was slowed by the other woman's four-year-old daughter, who had tearfully resented the idea of being left behind at home, and annoyed her mother. She was now being made to walk as a kind of punishment to deter her from insisting on coming along another time. At first, the little girl walked briskly, very likely enjoying the fact that she was not being carried. But that didn't last long. Soon she slowed down, complaining that her ankles hurt. Her mother merely told her sharply that if she did not walk she would be left behind.

The little girl tried out of fear to quicken her steps, but soon broke down. Her mother stood angrily over her. The girl, seeing this, gave a sharp cry of dismay that sent pain through Pokuwaa's heart. She could not understand the woman's attitude.

'Why not pick her up? You mustn't let her cry,' she said.

'I can't carry her,' the other shouted. 'She is as heavy as lead.'

'I wonder why some of these children don't come to me. I will handle one like an egg,' Pokuwaa said. The woman was very much amused.

'I don't think you will. You will get fed up soon enough,' she said. 'I thought the same way when I hadn't had my first child. Then came the first, the second, the third. This one is the fifth. And now I can't even eat. They take life out of me. Sometimes I get fed up with life, the way the children give me trouble.'

Pokuwaa listened to her carefully. Was all this true? Here she was equally fed up and bored with life because she had no child. If a mother was fed up when she had children, then what life was this?

'You mothers sometimes behave as if you don't have any pain at the birth of your children,' she said.

They continued their walk, the other explaining, 'We do, but it needs, perhaps, patience. Well, Ɛbɔ yebehyia.' They were parting, the woman having reached the branch off to her farm.

As Pokuwaa walked on, she could still hear her shouting

33

at the little girl to keep up her pace. She envied the company which the child provided, wishing she had someone to talk to.

This year the rains became particularly heavy. The compounds were muddy and the paths thick with weed. People were forced to stay in bed till late in the day. They could do nothing more than come out briefly to eat. Families were grateful for their reserves of corn, for food was running short, and they could not go to their farms.

Pokuwaa made a small fire in her hut on which to roast corn. Kwadwo spent many hours with her sitting at the fire. She specially enjoyed the playful struggles between them for the little food that she could prepare.

When the sky cleared one day, Pokuwaa took the opportunity to visit Koramoa. She found her cooking. Her child, now a toddler, was waddling about, splashing mud over himself, falling down and struggling up again. He was clearly enjoying learning to walk and refused to sit down. When Koramoa caught him to wash his feet he let out shrill cries and wriggled to get down.

Koramoa regretted that the days had made their meetings so irregular, and complained about the naughtiness of her child.

'We must try and keep in touch,' said Pokuwaa, 'as human beings should do.'

'You are very nice,' praised Koramoa. 'I was thinking of coming to see you, but what with the rains and this boy . . . I want to discuss with you Kofi Deede's behaviour recently. He has started giving me trouble again over women. Only last night, when I was sitting here waiting for him, someone

34

came to tell me that he was in the hut of Akosua Seewaa. I went there and caught them together.'

'So where is he now?' asked Pokuwaa.

'He has gone out again,' said her friend. 'He is so ashamed he cannot look at my face. You see, I had seen him with her once, but when I asked him questions he denied having anything to do with her. Now I hear he wants to marry her. If that is true I shall divorce him.'

'Oh, Afua Koramoa, be a little patient,' Pokuwaa counselled.

'I have tried patience for too long,' Koramoa retorted. 'First it was for a child. Now I have a child and I am not happy. I shall leave him.'

'With your child you should be a happy woman,' urged Pokuwaa. 'You leave Kofi Dede to his ways. He will cool off soon enough.'

'No,' her friend insisted. 'I can't even eat well. Look, I haven't eaten today.'

By the time Pokuwaa left however she had managed to calm Koramoa down and got her to agree to stay and watch.

'He will have to eat there,' said Koramoa as an afterthought. 'I will not cook for him.'

'If you do that it will be like sending him like a gift of yam to Seewaa. She will cook and eat without saying thanks to you.' Pokuwaa knew these words would make an impression on her friend.

As she stepped outside, she saw Kofi Dede coming home. Passing him she whispered, 'Stop what you are doing,' and walked on.

# Chapter Five

ONE night the whole village woke up to roars of raging fire. Kwadwo ran out to investigate and came back with the news that lightning had struck the Wawa tree outside the village.

'Hei, that is a bad omen,' said Pokuwaa.

'A rare thing,' Kwadwo agreed. 'Perhaps the gods are angry.'

This was everybody's opinion. The gods were wreaking vengeance. For days the tall tree burnt sending flames high up over the village. At night the streets were lit by the flames. Children who were normally fearful of the night ran up and down the streets jumping in ecstasy. But the fire caused serious concern in the older community. They consulted oracles and all the women of Brenhoma were requested to cook for the pacification of ancestral spirits. Pokuwaa was there in the area of the meeting of elders which decided this. She knew that the men's decisions had really come from the women and travelled with them to the meeting place. She said to a man who was standing near her, 'I don't think all that needs to be said has been said. We must look for the person who was the cause of this. We were lucky that the lightning hit a tree. If it had hit a hut where would we be?'

'You are right,' said the man. 'I will put that point across.'

'Press it home,' urged Pokuwaa. 'If we leave it as it is, whoever the person may be may commit a similar offence and the anger will come upon us in a more disastrous way.'

When the man spoke, the elders assured him that this investigation was not being neglected. 'The feeding of our ancestral spirits,' they explained, 'is to pacify them in the meantime.'

Pokuwaa took part in the ceremony which attained the proportions of a feast. She took her food to the ancestral home and it was placed on the ground. Why was food for the departed always placed on the ground? Well, the elders knew what was best. She watched the oldest member of the clan take a calabashful of palm wine and pour it on the ground requesting the gods and ancestors not to visit Brenhoma with any disease. Someone added, 'And may all barren women bear children so that, when you come to our home to visit us, you will always find someone here to give you something to eat.'

Pokuwaa nodded assent. She had more than one reason why she was interested in the ceremony to keep the gods' anger off the village. Supposing in their vengeance they made her personal sacrifices unsuccessful? She bent down her head in her own prayer as the food was being distributed to the seventy-seven gods of Brenhoma. Fufu was placed in morsels and soup poured over them. Each god's name was evoked, and the officiating elder said:

'Feed from our hands this day and grant our requests. We are your servants and your guests. Your commands stand supreme. Never visit us with any disease. Send it away over the high seas. Bring us abundance!'

After this everybody took some of the food and ate sitting in groups. The men sat round pots of palm wine drinking and singing, as it was manly to do.

This day Kwadwo had joined his own people in his ancestral home. As Pokuwaa watched the men drinking, she wondered what was happening to him, and went out to fetch him home.

# Chapter Six

THE rains eventually became gradual, permitting the ground to dry out. The village was filthy with rubbish that the currents had deposited in many places. People spent time cleaning up that and the slimy green moss that had grown and spread in the lanes and streets. There was also much repair work for them, for walls had collapsed and even some foundations had been washed away.

Pokuwaa disliked the smell of rotten things around. She hated filth of any sort. She took great care with the cleaning up of her own house. With the rains easing off, market days in Brenhoma became more busy again, and people looked forward each week to the meetings with their friends from neighbouring villages, which the rains had interrupted.

Sometimes Pokuwaa went to the market taking peppers or plantains or cola nuts. She didn't need to make many cowries, because after all she only had herself and her mother to take care of. She kept the cowries she made in a brass pan in which she kept her important belongings; her earrings and a ring which her father had given her when she married her first husband.

One night when she and Kwadwo were together, she started counting her cowries.

Kwadwo said, 'Is that to show me how rich you are?'

'Oh,' said Pokuwaa gaily, 'don't you know? I was rich even when I was only ten years old.'

'You can take me for a fool, if you like,' laughed Kwadwo.

'It's true,' she said. 'The old chief liked me and used to give me gifts. At the age of ten I had two hundred cowries of my own.'

'Well,' Kwadwo ridiculed, 'why didn't you buy yourself a slave or two? A hundred cowries were enough to buy one, weren't they?'

'And what would I do with a slave? Those who have them are constantly having to deal with stubbornness and rebellion, are they not? All I want is a child of my own blood.'

'True,' sighed Kwadwo.

'And I really ought to be getting on with it. They say it is always best to get what you have to do done in time.' Kwadwo sighed again.

'You never know what will befall,' Pokuwaa said brokenly. She meant much more than her lips would say, and Kwadwo understanding this convention of unfinished statements tried to relax her painful thoughts.

'As for you Ashantis,' he said trying to be casual, 'you are so fond of unfinished sentences and code words.'

'Well,' said Pokuwaa, brightening up, 'it is because we Ashantis have ears to hear and understand our own secret language.'

'It had to be so. We are a warring people, and you can never tell whether or not there is a spy around. Why, in cases of distress and emergency we can speak to each other with our heads, our feet, or by merely twitching and turning our bodies.'

'Yes,' said Pokuwaa approvingly. Then she was quiet for a while. 'Actually, when I said you never can tell, I was thinking about my father's death.'

'You notice I haven't ever talked with you about it,' said Kwadwo. 'I know it must have been sad for you.'

Pokuwaa wanted to tell him all about it. 'It occurred on a Fofie. He died in a distant village several miles from Brenhoma. He had been taken there to be cured by a fetish priest. My mother went with him. He could not walk, and was carried in his hammock. Oh, he was so weak. But the priest had promised he would save him if we got him there alive. We had wanted him to come down to Brenhoma, but he refused to, because he said the witch who was eating up father was in this village, and whatever he could do would be nullified by her. So it was better to get the sick man away. My mother took father away from Brenhoma without notice to anyone. Four men went along to carry my father in stages, two at a time, on that long trek.

'I felt uneasy as I waved goodbye to them. I would particularly miss father and knew he would miss me too. I am his only daughter, and we were good friends. He gave me all the good things in the house. He named me after his mother. As I grew up he dropped my name Pokuwaa and simply called me mother. I was delighted with that because it made me feel grown up. In return I did everything for him, getting him his water for his bath, and making the mashed meal he liked so much.

41

'Then that sacred Friday I was waiting until noon to go to the market. I was sweeping when the messenger arrived suddenly. My father was dead, he said. Well—I looked at him standing there in mourning cloth, carrying the state sword—and my heart hurt me.

'Anyway, I went into my room and picked up a few things for my journey. It took a day's walk through the forest. If it hadn't been a day of distress I would have enjoyed the monkeys and chimpanzees. Kofi Dafo went with me. I was full of anxiety. I wished mother had permitted me to go with them when they left. But who would have taken care of the house? We brought father back to Brenhoma and buried him. If the dead could hear, he would have come back to life to comfort me. You know at that time of sharp pain we the living wish that if our dead can't wake they should take us along with them.'

'That is true,' said Kwadwo quietly.

'Does anybody know what exists in the ghost world? At Asamando? We have nothing to give us a clue, have we? Do people who say we are sent to another world where there is no trouble and no suffering really know?'

'Well, we certainly believe it,' said Kwadwo earnestly.

'If we thought they weren't still existing somewhere would we serve food to our ancestors? Would our state be so diligent about the rites of the black stools in which the souls of our dead chiefs reside, and which permit us to communicate with them?

'And yet it is true that nobody comes back here from that hidden kingdom. What can we do? We will believe the priests who speak of the happiness or anger of our departed ones—and carry out our sacrifices,' said Pokuwaa wearily.

She got up, and when she spoke again the sound was less sad. 'I sometimes wonder if I would really have wanted to go with my father as I said in my weeping.'

# Chapter Seven

THE priests said that the heavy rains were a sign of a plentiful harvest, and everybody looked forward to the time of the new yams. Pokuwaa's mother was one of the women at Brenhoma who supported the forecast of the priests with emphasis.

'The oracles don't lie,' she declared. 'When I was a young woman about the age of our neighbour's daughter Akosua Mansa, the rains came down so hard that we thought the grasshoppers would go blind. We were kept shut up in our homes for a long time. After that, you should have seen the harvest. The sight of our farms filled us with happiness. Plantain and bananas ripened to rottenness. Why? Because we couldn't bring all that food home. Everybody had enough to eat. All we needed was salt.'

'In that case,' said Pokuwaa, 'we should really see something this time. The rains have caused the earth to ooze with water.'

'Yes, all the streams of Brenhoma are overflowing,' confirmed her mother.

Pokuwaa talked about the stream that was now running on the eastern part of her farm. She frequently made a fire near it and halfway through her work she stopped to cook her food there. The stream gave her pleasure.

Her own yams were growing well. She spent time walking among the mounds, uprooting with the care of a herbalist the weeds and climbers which were trying to choke the tender yam shoots. A spirit of hopefulness was abroad in Brenhoma.

'If the year comes round to meet us,' people said, 'we shall have a real harvest with which to celebrate it.' They even thought that their farms looked promising enough to yield new yams well in advance of their Odwira festival.

But this hope soon faded because a sudden drought came, and the sun beat down, withering up the crops. It lasted for weeks, scorching the earth, and leaving many trees naked. The water dried up in the streams. Pokuwaa dug holes in her stream and a little water bubbled out but only for a few days. She had to carry water again to her farm. Watching the yam tendrils withering, and the young roots rotting in the mounds was very painful. Talk in Brenhoma became more anxious when the time arrived for the Odwira festival to be announced. What were they going to celebrate it with? they moaned.

The evening that the day of the festival was announced, Pokuwaa, her mother and Kwadwo Fordwuo were sitting comforting each other in Pokuwaa's courtyard around a log fire.

'What are we going to do?' asked Pokuwaa. 'It's only one month to the festival and no yams.'

Her mother said, 'There is time yet, Pokuwaa. Besides,

some people's good luck saved their crops from destruction. There will be a few yams at least.'

'Is there not some chance that they have wrongly calculated the date this year?' asked Pokuwaa hopefully.

Kwadwo took the clay pipe he was smoking out of his mouth and laughed heartily. 'Oh, Pokuwaa, there are three fetish priests doing the calculation.'

'But they can all be wrong,' she insisted.

'The street crier's announcement is right,' said her mother. 'The day is Awukudae without any doubt.'

'Don't forget,' added Kwadwo, 'that when the chief sits in state at the Odwira durbar, that bag of corn he receives among the gifts that day is something the priests guard with great care. They don't hang the emptied bag in the corner of our sacred grove for nothing. Because we all expect them to calculate the date of our festival correctly, they scrutinise each grain of corn that is dropped in every day. They know when there are three hundred and fifty grains of corn in it. No self-respecting priest would cause an announcement to be made unless he is sure it is one month to the festival.'

'Listen,' said Pokuwaa. 'I have heard it said that there was a time when some mistake was made.'

'It's not a lie,' her mother said, smiling as she remembered. 'A mischievous son of the chief priest at that time threw several extra grains of corn into the bag, due to his father's lack of vigilance. When the day of the final counting came, the priest certainly had a problem. Brenhoma was furious with him. He was disgraced and deposed. We called him the lying prophet. If custom had been taken to its utmost, he and his sons and daughters would have been killed. As it was,

the young man who had thrown the town into this confusion
was nearly torn to pieces.'

'Did you celebrate the festival that year?'

'Yes. But we weren't as happy as we should have been. We
all knew the time was wrong. The yams were still far from
ready to be dug out of their mounds.'

Kwadwo, trying to be cheerful, said, 'Let's hope that
now, with three priests counting, each with a separate bag
to enable him to check on the others, that such mistakes
are truly avoided.'

'Let's hope so,' said Pokuwaa.


Tum tum bam, tum bam bam, tum tum
tu tum, tu tum bam.

People had only barely recovered from the drought
when the drums, Fontonfrom, Kete, Odensew and Adowa,
called upon the people to keep the night-long vigil of the
Odwira.

Pokuwaa, who had been dozing, woke up to the sound of
loud applause in the village, hailing the drums.

'So it is vigil night,' she said, shaking her husband awake,
and drawing his attention to the clapping of hands in the
distance.

'Ah, the fetish rites,' Kwadwo announced. It was moon-
light outside. They lit the lamp that had gone out. Kwadwo
noticed at this instant the cracks in the walls and said, 'New
year. I must patch up those cracks for you.'

'Don't bother about them now,' Pokuwaa laughed. 'Just
now, it's the vigil that's important.'

47

They were getting ready to go out when Nsamangoro came passing by.

'Listen to the elderly people doing their game through the streets,' said Pokuwaa.

They listened to the single and clanging nnawuta, and the coarse singing of the old folk.

'Old people,' said Pokuwaa, 'they can't help singing in discord.'

'It doesn't matter,' Kwadwo answered. 'They know the traditions. If they weren't there to pass them on at our gatherings and feasts, how would the young ones learn?'

As Pokuwaa listened to the fading melody she said, 'It won't be long before that is my group.'

'Come, let us go,' said Kwadwo, adjusting his cloth. They went out into the village. The drums seemed to hold the whole place together in one expanse of peaceful melody. Deep-moving notes filled the cool night air.

Tonight, there seemed to be about eight drumming groups, and new variations of rhythms in the air. Pokuwaa observed that when she was a girl there were fewer dances. Kwadwo remarked, 'This is the time in the village when you get the meaning of "If one generation is dead another has come." Today's generation has become very interested in drumming and dancing. Here they come.'

A drumming group approached them, their dancers vigorously throwing themselves in the air, and then rolling in the very centre of the music. In another street Kwadwo and Pokuwaa came upon wrestlers displaying their skills and showing off the powers of new juju they had acquired.

On their way to the silk cotton tree they saw and joked about the many lovers at the street corners.

'It appears that everyone comes to the vigil with a purpose,' said Pokuwaa. 'For the drummers it is always a chance to drum as if to burst their drums.'

'And the lovers come to whisper sweetness out of their hearts. Look at them.'

In the shadows of the silk cotton trees many of them were to be seen.

'They will make bold resolutions for the coming year, and then we'll see after that.'

'There are also those whose hands are still empty, looking for someone.'

'Oh, yes, they know what to do though. They'll mix with the crowds, taking care to stand next to girls. Those are usually the shy ones. Such boys and girls have a way of just appearing beside each other as if they didn't know that there is anything between them. But in the next six hours, before the sun comes up, their eyes will meet all right.'

'Were you one of the shy ones, Pokuwaa?'

'Don't make fun of me, Kwadwo Fordwuo,' Pokuwaa laughed delightedly.

A group of six or seven girls suddenly ran gleefully out from somewhere, already dancing towards another drumming group which was approaching from the furthest end of the town.

'This night does make the girls lively,' said Kwadwo.

'Let them be,' Pokuwaa said. 'Isn't it the only night in the year when they can stay out a whole night without getting

49

queried? You just look at the moon. Who wouldn't feel lively on such a beautiful night?'

'When tomorrow finds us, we shall weep.'

'Yes,' said Pokuwaa, 'we shall weep indeed. That is the custom.'

Koramoa found them and came running to them. They wandered round until Kwadwo said he needed rest for his duties in his father's house in the morning. They all walked home together and sat for a while in the yard chatting about the amusing things going on in the village that night.

'You women will keep me here until sunrise,' said Kwadwo when he rose. 'I must close my eyes a little.' He went into Pokuwaa's room, asking her if she wasn't going to sleep that night.

'Koramoa and I will talk a little longer,' she said.

Their talk wove in and out of their childhood, and of festivals gone by and happily shared by both.

'And the old chief,' said Koramoa, drawing a story out of Pokuwaa.

'Yes, poor man. He died and went his way. He was very attentive to me, wasn't he, Koramoa?'

'Are you surprised? You were a beautiful child, and grew more so.'

'Didn't other dancers receive gifts from him? Hadn't he seen several other beauties? Weren't you included? He had a giving hand. When he sat in state at the feast and watched us dance, didn't you also receive from him a cowrie and a yam?'

Koramoa laughed. 'Pokuwaa, you should also say that even before you could dance, from the age of five, he gave

50

you a gift at each festival. And when we danced I suspect he gave you twice as much as we received.'

They both laughed heartily at this, for it was so.

'You are a good dancer,' said Koramoa. 'That is true. You were already good at ten years old.'

'Ah,' said Pokuwaa, 'I'm not so young now.'

But the topic was too sweet to drop.

'The old man helped to make me a good dancer by those praises he showered on me at festivals. I used to practise hard learning our best skills. I always went to a festival with a new step or a new turn.'

'I know,' said Koramoa. 'And didn't the drummers know how to play special rhythms for the dark girl with the fine eyebrows whom the chief admired so much? They did it with the enthusiasm of servants pleasing their master. And drummers should be pleased with a girl who dances with all her body, like you.'

'Sometimes when dancing Kete, Asonko, Odensew and Adowa, I would forget about everybody there. Only the dancing. It enters my body, and I forget everything else.'

'Ha, in this world we don't know what is coming. Imagine how it was put about that, without doubt, in no time, the chief would ask for your hand.'

'Yes, when I myself couldn't say I loved him. On no occasion did he attract me. I always called him Nana, even in my own head. I sat at his feet with his servants when I went to the Ahenfie. It was mother who used to send me there. I think she did it when she was in need. "Whatever you ask of him, he will do," she said. "You don't even have to ask, he will give you anyway." So I went.'

'You see, you didn't know it, but all the time she had her own understanding. There is always a hook in the mind of an elder.'

'He called me such affectionate names that made me hide my face. "Otwewaa Pokuwaa, Ahwenie, you can have what you want. How many cowries shall I give you? Do you want cloth?" If I managed to whisper three cowries, he would give me more. And I would run away from there and give the cowries to my mother. Sometimes when his hunters brought him meat, he sent servants here with special cuts for us, even the parts he himself was entitled to.'

'You wept very bitterly when he died,' said Koramoa.

'I can't explain why I cried so when I heard the news. Whenever I stopped crying, I felt a heaviness in my throat, and the tears fell and fell. For days I lost my taste for food. I was so young. It was my first real contact with sorrow, losing someone I counted upon.'

'We children were not permitted to go to the burial,' said Koramoa.

'No, and mother had to stay by my side comforting me.'

'He got good burial and good mourning,' said Koramoa. 'Fifty years of good and prosperous reign.'

'Brenhoma doesn't forget him,' added Pokuwaa. 'Through his wisdom, the wars ceased.'

'Even peace was made with the people of Domakwae with whom we share boundaries, is that not right?'

'He was a young man when he was seated on the stool and he combined his energy and his wisdom in developing Brenhoma,' said Pokuwaa. 'Did you know our present Ahenfie was built by him?'

'In Brenhoma we know everything about him. Oh, Pokuwaa, times have changed really. Do the girls of today even have an ear for the drum?'

Pokuwaa became enthusiastic. 'I was dancing one day when I heard the drums talking to me. The big Fontonfrom led them. I stopped and changed my steps and shook my head.'

'So you did,' said Koramoa, clapping at the thought of it. 'All of us applauded.'

'It was a real test of my dancing,' said Pokuwaa.

'And then the people shouted, "Odamani akodaa wo sa a ma wo ti mmo nko. Ma wo ti mmo nko."'

Pokuwaa threw her head back laughing and sweeping her cloth in between her legs. That was it. Girl of the times, when you dance shake, shake your head. Shake your head.

'You shook it, Pokuwaa. You shook it really hard.'

'Listen, isn't that the rhythm we are hearing now?'

'Yes, the drummers are hitting it out.'

They rushed childishly out of the house again, and joined the other people who had also been attracted to run to the centre of town. There, everybody seemed to be running. And what an uproar! Pokuwaa and Koramoa pushed their way through. In the centre of the dancing a young chimpanzee was dancing too—if that was dancing he did jumping around instead of drawing his feet to the rhythms of the drums. For the first time in a very long time, Pokuwaa found herself laughing from her stomach itself. She laughed so well that she felt pains in her side.

When they wished each other good sleep and went home, the night was far gone.

53

When morning came, Brenhoma had turned to wailing. Pokuwaa, wearing her best Kuntunkuni, joined the people for the general mourning for the ancestors. Their mood caught up with the children who also joined hands and simulated a weeping session, singing dirges and drumming. Nobody cooked that day. After the general mourning people went to weep their personal dead. Pokuwaa mourned her own father. Her mother spent nearly all day by her side, bound to her in one bond of weeping and fasting. In the afternoon they discussed their plans for the following day. Her mother asked her to get her things together for cooking a meal to send to her father's house. 'I am sure his spirit will be present in Brenhoma tomorrow,' she said, 'and he would like a meal.' Pokuwaa agreed. 'If only there were more yams,' she worried. 'We are only left with old yams from last season.'

Her mother rose, went to the kitchen, and returned with two fine yams. 'I managed to get these,' she said, giving them to her. 'They are enough for cooking for our dead.'

'So tomorrow are we holding the feasting day of our festival?' asked Pokuwaa.

'Ah, we will try,' said her mother dispiritedly.

'Without a harvest?' Pokuwaa continued.

'Some people have a little. And what they have, we all have,' said the old lady. 'Our dead will eat, and that is enough. Those who look after the world will look after it. The harvest is late, and there is not much hope of abundance. But we will give thanks just the same.'

'There won't be many gifts when the chief sits in state tomorrow; not many gifts this year,' added Pokuwaa.

'It doesn't matter,' replied her mother. 'Custom is custom.

54

He will sit in state. And we will all go and swear to him, and even we old ones will shuffle our withered legs in the dances. We have set aside this time for joy in this wearying life. He will sit in state, Pokuwaa.'

'It is good,' her daughter agreed.

'And however distressed we are,' said the old lady, 'we will at least not be too destitute to present him with our customary bag of corn. I am going to sleep.'

Because of the fasting that day Pokuwaa woke up late in the night feeling very hungry. She stole out into the kitchen, and groped round the pots to see if there was anything left over to eat. She thought she heard a little thud, but at the same time her fingers dipped into food and she started scooping it up from the pot into her mouth. She was trying to grope round for something to sit on when her left hand felt the nose of a dog. The frightened animal gave a sharp yelp, and Pokuwaa snatched her hand away.

'Adwoa Pokuwaa, is that you stealing out in the dark to eat on fasting day?' her mother called from the gateway, and laughed.

Pokuwaa had to laugh too. 'The dog that caught me also came thinking there was nobody around,' she said. 'Haven't you gone to sleep?'

'I am talking with the night,' said her mother.

Pokuwaa returned to her room. Kwadwo was fast asleep, stretched across the bed. She pushed him carefully to one side and stretched herself beside him. But sleep didn't come. She thought of the prayers that would be said in the morning, especially the prayer of the priestesses as they went round the village sprinkling the ritual yam.

'The year has come round, great Odomankoma.
Never can we thank you for your deeds and blessing
    for us.
Tano Kofi and all the seventy-seven gods of Brenhoma.
Come now and eat from our hands and bless your
    people.
Let all who are ill get well.
Let all who are barren bear children.
Let all who are impotent find remedy.
Don't let them go blind or paralysed.
We all beseech happiness.
Let us have it.'

She saw her own hand lifted up like the priestesses'. This
was the prayer she too wanted to offer—and she wished
she could augment it with words to suit her personal cir-
cumstances.

# Chapter Eight

THE passing of the Odwira seemed to take away the life in Brenhoma that year. Many people, with nothing but odd jobs to do in their homes, spent time sleepily under the silk cotton tree waiting for the yams to get ready for harvesting.

Pokuwaa decided to use some of these idle days in building a new fireplace for herself. She took her basket and hoe and fetched home some red earth from the outskirts of the village. She mixed and moulded the earth, shaping the three miniature hills of the hearth with the care of a potter. It took her three days, at the end of which she found that her food basket had run empty. She must go to Disemi to her farm and bring home whatever foodstuffs she could find.

It was noon when she started out with her basket on her head.

'Mother, I shall come back soon.'

'Come back in time for us to visit Maame Yaa Manu,' her mother said. 'I understand she fell down last night and broke her thigh bone.'

'Oh, is that so?' Pokuwaa was really sorry.

'Yes,' said her mother. 'We must never pray for old age to

come. It is a disease.' She took a few steps to the gate to see her daughter off.

As she approached the farm, Pokuwaa saw vultures in the sky. At first there weren't many of them, but they were acting as if there was some prey around. They hovered in the air and lowered themselves down. Presently they came in sixes and tens, swarming. She noticed when she reached her farm that the birds were collecting in the thicker part of the forest next door to her. She knew that it was a good hiding place for rats, but the birds were so plentiful that she thought she would get closer to them to see what was attracting them. Whatever it was, the smell from it was very bad. Carefully she prised her way through the tangled bushes with her cutlass, but the vultures heard her approach. They gave shrill cries and went up in a cloud of tawny wings, leaving a carcass behind them.

What Pokuwaa saw made her turn back with a sharp cry herself. There before her lay the body of a man. Flies were buzzing round it. It was the stench from its decomposition that she had smelled. She covered her face with her hands and stumbled back. There were scratches on her limbs and her skirt was torn when she reached her farm. She snatched up her basket, spilled the water in her gourd and ran back home.

Her mind was in great commotion. How did that dead body come to be there? It did occasionally happen that one man wanted to face another in combat and invited his opponent to the bush where they would be alone and the stronger would batter the weaker one to death. They would not be permitted to do this at home. Anyone who accepted such a fight knew that it would be carried out brutally until death. Pokuwaa remembered that she had seen blood on the leaves. If this was a combat, then perhaps the other man who got away did so with serious injuries. And who was he? There were no eyes in the body she had seen. Had the birds eaten them? Was that thing a club she'd seen lying by? A weapon? She hurried on.

As she got near Brenhoma it flashed upon her that if she went home with an empty basket she would attract attention and have to answer questions. 'Brenhoma is not like other places,' she said breathlessly. 'In other places if you break news of a disaster like this, people are prepared to assist. In Brenhoma I'm going to have to answer unending questions, head search parties, stand before a meeting of elders, who will listen and either let me have my head's innocence, or accuse me of having a hand in it. What am I going to do? There are snares; and if a meeting disbelieves me, I am in trouble.'

Still wondering how to decide, she stopped and collected a few sticks of firewood so that she could pass through the village carrying a normal bundle.

She was very nervous as she walked along. She threw the load down in the courtyard, and running into her room threw herself on the floor with a big sigh.

'Adwoa Pokuwaa,' called her mother from the kitchen. 'Don't you even greet me when you return from the farm?'

Pokuwaa couldn't answer. She couldn't bring herself to say anything, although she could hear the old lady's voice whining in the kitchen.

'You know I cannot bend properly,' the old lady was

59

saying. 'I have to get along anyhow I can with a stick when the pain takes me these days. And yet as soon as I'd had my bath and scrubbed my feet with extra care, I came and swept round the place. "It will lift Pokuwaa's heart up," I said. But she came and showed no appreciation.'

Pokuwaa heard her mother coming near and asking, 'And was that an empty basket you brought in?' She didn't answer.

'Pokuwaa! Pokuwaa!' the old lady called at the door. Then, seeing her daughter sprawling on the floor, she hobbled in alarmed, put her hand on her back and shook her violently. 'What has happened to you?' Pokuwaa could hear the tenderness in that question. 'Are you ill? You have never done this before. Something is surely wrong.'

'Mother.'

'What is wrong, Ahwenee? Tell me. You are ill, are you not?'

'No, I'm not ill,' she answered.

'Did anything happen at the farm?'

Pokuwaa's body was shaking now. Tears began rolling down her face. She hit her head with her hands as if to smash it. Her mother moved restlessly, unable to look at her pain, and yet trying not to force her to speak.

'What an end for a human being!' sobbed Pokuwaa.

'What are you saying? Tell me all. What is there that you cannot tell me? If you can't tell me whom can you tell?' Her mother sounded desperate. 'She is my mother,' thought Pokuwaa.

'I have seen something really terrible,' she blurted out at last.

'What? A ghost?'

'A dead man, in the forest near my farm. Oh, mother, it was terrible.'

When the old woman heard the story through, she heaved a sigh and shifted away from Pokuwaa. Her face was set as if she had heard a murderer confess to her.

'I think this is a very serious matter,' she said slowly. 'I feel that we should keep it to ourselves. We will not mention it to anybody else.'

But the secret filled the house like a heavy mist.

# Chapter Nine

'PEOPLE of Brenhoma! Elders, young ones! I bring you greetings from the chief!' The village crier's voice and gong, resounding together through Brenhoma at the quiet of sunset, brought people out of their homes in a hurry.

The announcement seemed to cut like a knife through Pokuwaa's tangled thoughts. As she fumbled about with nervous fingers for various items of clothing, she could hear the shout of people in one neighbourhood, followed by the closing kon, kon, kon, of the crier's gong.

'He has delivered his message,' thought Pokuwaa, feeling that although she hadn't heard it, she knew what the subject was. Soon the gong was sounding in another neighbourhood.

Pokuwaa ran out towards the group that was gathering in her own neighbourhood. She noticed that the usual babble of speculation with which people awaited the arrival of the village crier was not evident today.

The silence troubled her and made her so busy with the thoughts in her head that, when the crier's gong clanged out to dismiss the listeners in the other street, she was startled.

The crier came stepping briskly along.

'People of Brenhoma. Elders and young! I bring you greetings from the chief. Every young man fit to walk is commanded to come out tomorrow at the first cock-crow to join in the search for Yaw Boakye. He failed to return home, and we have not heard from him since last Monday. Whoever doesn't turn up will be punished by the great oath.' Kon! kon! kon!

The crowd he left behind him, as he strode briskly on, was a silent one. When it quietly broke apart, Pokuwaa lingered round, wishing that someone else would make a comment. She knew why she herself dared not talk, dared not say anything to suggest that she had found a group of vultures feasting on a human corpse near her farm. The crier's voice came echoing from another street.

'Tomorrow,' Pokuwaa said, 'someone will find the body and save me the trouble that reporting it myself would bring to me.' But she also wished she could step forward boldly and tell the chief, 'I know where the body is.' Would they believe she was telling all she knew? She heaved a sigh and turned to walk back home.

A mother with her baby on her back greeted her, and said, 'Ɛbɔ! What did the crier say? I wasn't able to get out in time.'

'It was about Boakye who has not returned home,' reported Pokuwaa.

'Oh, Pokuwaa,' said the woman despairingly. 'I saw him only last Sunday.'

'Yes, I believe you,' said Pokuwaa with a sigh.

'Oh, Boakye, he was such a courageous man, such a soldier.'

63

Pokuwaa only nodded. She dared not encourage a conversation.

That night she lay in bed carefully retracing her steps to take a second look at the half-eaten corpse. Sleep mercifully came to her, but her dreams dragged her back again to the farm. She could see herself there, investigating a scent that was all pervasive. Suddenly four men who were hiding behind the trees seized her. She screamed so loudly that Kwadwo elbowed her awake.

'What is the matter?' His voice was sleepy but full of alarm.

'Er, nothing,' said Pokuwaa hoarsely. 'I was dreaming.'

'It must be a terrible dream.'

'Yes, seeing terrible things,' she said, drawing nearer to him and pulling the cover over her. Kwadwo threw his arm over her as well, saying that he needed to sleep undisturbed in order to wake up at the first cock-crow when the search would begin.

Pokuwaa's thoughts did not rest. Grateful to have Kwadwo close, even though he was asleep, she clutched him tight. And when the drums suddenly burst out, she felt a tenseness that was hard to contain.

'It isn't dawn yet,' she whispered. 'He must not go out there yet.'

The drums jerked Kwadwo awake. They were the Asafo drums, saying,

> 'Who is the brave?
> Come out, come out
> Men of Brenhoma, come out.

64

We are calling for responsible men.
Barima Otu Brempong
Is calling for those who are men.'

The palm mat hanging outside her door rustled. Pokuwaa cried, 'Kwadwo, come back,' and ran out after him, but he was hurrying away to join the other men.

'Kwadwo,' she cried again, trying to catch up with him. He halted, and walked back to her. 'I don't think it is dawn yet,' she said. 'You need not go so soon.'

'They are gathering,' said Kwadwo. 'Can't you hear the drums?'

Indeed she could; those deep tones that always succeeded in warming the blood of the brave.

'I am not a coward,' said Kwadwo.

'Go then,' Pokuwaa said, 'but keep to the outskirts of the village. Don't go into the deep forest—not yet, for it is still night.' That was all she could manage to say; and she wanted to say, 'Don't go near my farm at Disemi, for the body of Yaw Boakye is waiting there, and it is an awful sight.'

She watched Kwadwo disappear in the uneasy light, his tall figure followed by her anxiety. For the next hour or more she heard the drums talking in the village meeting ground. The men were obviously waiting for the dawn.

When Kwadwo arrived he saw that he was among the first few to gather round the drummers.

'The moon deceived us,' the drummers explained cheerfully.

The chief drummer said, 'When my eyes cleared, this whole village was gleaming with light. How was I to know the moon was not telling the time right?' Everybody laughed. More men started to arrive. Kwadwo, trying to keep himself awake, took over the twin gong and played it. He used to know the instrument well, having played it at festivals years back when he was a member of the Odesew group. Now, he noticed that he hit a few wrong notes. His friends noticed it too, and laughed at him.

'Yes, I can see that I must get back to regular practice,' he said, handing back the gong.

By now the gathering had swelled. Many men were in their farming clothes, carrying their cutlasses ready for action.

When the first cock crew, Kwadwo thought he could have slept a little longer as Pokuwaa had advised. He edged out of the crowd to sit against a wall, and having no trouble about falling asleep was soon dozing. He was still sitting there asleep when the march began.

At the edge of the village, the Asafo captain arranged the men in groups. Moving forward with the group he himself was leading, he said, 'This scene brings me memories of the last war. I was an energetic young man then, fighting alongside my father. My father acknowledged my bravery by bringing home a slave girl to become the wife with whom I now have six children and all those grandchildren. It is as long ago as that. Then the old chief came to agreement with the people of Domakwae, and the wars ceased.'

It was at this point that Kwadwo came running to join the men. He was greeted with loud hoots. If they knew his whole story, they would have poked worse fun at him. Pokuwaa, in her restlessness, had picked up her water pot intending to walk with the men as far as the river to fetch water. When she reached the meeting ground, she found someone propped against the wall. She reeled back, threw her pot down, and started screaming, 'A ghost! A ghost!'

Startled, Kwadwo opened his eyes and jumped to his feet. He did not waste time to inquire about the screaming. He ran straight out of the village, and following the direction of the drums found the men on the way to Amantua. It is not surprising that he made no explanations for his lateness.

Many of the young men in the search had never seen war, and therefore were beginners at tactical manœuvre. They walked on talking excitedly until the captain sternly called them to a halt.

'What kind of Asafo are you?' he said. 'Who told you you could march to a search in this manner? Break your group up into twos, and search every bush, every tree buttress and every hole. Arrange to meet perhaps a mile ahead of you, to discuss your experience as a group, and then continue.'

The young men accepted his authority, got into formation, and started the search in earnest. On the advance, the searchers' minds were held together and directed towards the centre by six drummers. The messages of encouragement sent out from time to time on the drums filled the whole forest, and kept the women left behind at home in anxious discussion. The alarm that Pokuwaa had raised there had brought even greater nervousness to the village. The women who had run out into the street when she shouted, had themselves heard footsteps thudding away towards the outskirts of the village, and they were ready to believe that it was indeed a ghost that Pokuwaa had seen.

An old woman said that ghosts don't go running in that

manner. But in many people's opinion, it was the ghost of Boakye that Pokuwaa had seen.

'He is dead,' they said.

'His ghost was visiting his birthplace, before setting out for Asaman.'

'And we are searching for him today. Oh, Boakye!'

Pokuwaa hung round the village like all the women. Inside her, she kept praying that Kwadwo would keep away from Disemi and save himself the distressing encounter.

The drums took the men further into the forest. The sun arose when they reached an area where the Ananse stream joined the Kunkum river. They had plucked oranges, pine-apples and bananas in the course of their search, which they now settled down in groups to eat. Each group seemed to have something to laugh about. In Kwadwo's group, one man coming upon a bush cat and its litter, had started screaming. His companions thought he had found Boakye. They closed in. He pointed to the spot, saying, 'There! There!' But all they found was the cat and its babies.

'Such cowards should not have come along with us,' said Kwadwo. They all laughed and continued to jeer at the poor man as they washed their faces and their feet to freshen themselves for the next stage of the search.

That day, they went as far as the Asamansua river, before they decided to give up.

Returning home, they found the women still hanging around with different versions of the ghost story to tell.

Kwadwo knew the truth. But how could he say that he had been sleeping when men were already on the march? When he took Pokuwaa home, he asked with a smile,

'Adwoa, do I bear any resemblance to Yaw Boakye?'

Pokuwaa looked at him and said, 'No, why do you ask such a question?'

'I only wanted to know,' he said, still smiling as he entered her room. This puzzled Pokuwaa, but he had a long story to tell her that night about the excitement of the search and she was willing to be diverted.

The search was much more exciting the following day. At the first cock-crow the men were already in the forest. The day before, one group had found the track of a boar. This was the reason for the early start. Carrying their palm torches high, they pursued the boar's track for some time, before they set a trap and retreated under some high bamboos to await the dawn.

The captain was still talking about Brenhoma's last attack on Domakwae. He said, 'Day was only just breaking, and we were on the march through the bush to surprise them. No news of our advance leaked out to them. We raided the village, carrying away goats and sheep, and women.'

One of the men said, 'And when you got the women did you throw your bow and arrow away, because your hands were full?'

'Capturing women is not easy at all,' said the captain. 'It doesn't matter how much courage you have, you need tact as well, and beauty.'

Everybody rolled with laughter at this.

'Yes, laugh,' said the captain. 'It is fitting that you do so. Looking at my bald head and missing teeth, you may well not imagine that I ever was handsome. But thirty years ago, I stood straight and whole. Let me tell you that the woman I caught in the war and wanted to carry away volunteered to follow me herself. She was captivated by my handsomeness. So pleased were we with each other, that we arranged our marriage on the way. Now, as a result of the manner in which the world has dragged us both about, none of you young men would think we had ever had any pleasure in our lives. Rise up. Let us move on.'

The men jumped into action, picking up the song the captain called,

> 'Men of Brenhoma, men of ancient dynasty,
> Men of brave ancestry!
> Tano Kofi's sons,
> We are not afraid.'

The search was progressing towards Disemi, when a strong odour alerted one group after the other. The groups pulled together towards the centre to confer.

If vultures flew so early in the morning, the men would have been spared the hard search that led to the source of the awful stench.

It was from Kwadwo's group that the alarm came at last. 'Wasps! wasps! Take care!' They all knew what that meant. A body had been found. That was the normal way to announce news of that nature during a search. The men closed in on what was left of the body.

A drum relayed a message immediately. 'People of Brenhoma. We mourn Boakye. We mourn Yaw Boakye. Condolences.'

Messengers were dispatched as well, to ask the chief to get the relatives of Boakye ready to receive him for burial.

# Chapter Ten

As mourners filed in and out of Yaw Boakye's family house, Adwoa Pokuwaa kept her seat by the entrance from where she watched the funeral proceedings with a far-away look in her eyes. Occasionally she felt the heat of a sudden gush of tears, or tasted their bitter salt. But she was not conscious of any desire to weep. The pain in her seemed to demand some other expression which she could not give. The wailing of other mourners which normally would have drawn her own tears, merely made her feel dry and desolate inside.

The smell of ferns and other strong herbs burning in the courtyard kept her constantly reminded of the remains assembled in the wooden coffin in the funeral room opposite her. She would stare at the rising curls of scented smoke for long moments, then at the coffin that was so still, and draw her cloth tightly round her shoulders and shiver. Her eyes would then rest on the more comforting sight of the bed on which different kinds of food were displayed with care in wooden trays and earthen bowls—Boakye's favourite dishes when he was alive, presented by his wife and sister.

'Man of the miserable end! Let him take a little com-

71

fort from that. If it is true what we believe, that on this day the spirit is home to prepare finally for the journey to the new world, let Yaw Boakye take comfort from this feast.'

There was drumming and dancing. Many men and women performed for Yaw Boakye. When his friends got into formation for his favourite group dance, they carefully left his position vacant and asked, 'Where is Boakye? Boakye, where are you?' It made a pathetic scene when the dance turned into a dance of weeping.

When Boakye's widows came in to give him the cowries which he would use to pay for his passage across the river into the spirit world, Pokuwaa felt like screaming. But she only drew her cloth tightly again round her, and dug her toes into the earth floor. 'When life has so rubbed you in misery, what do you do? Where do you turn?'

The sun was setting, its red glow would soon deepen and persist for a considerable length of time before darkness finally closed in. No shadows are cast at the time of sunset glow, therefore no one need fear that the coffin's shadow will fall across him to drive him closer to his own death.

The time for burying Yaw Boakye had come. As if this was what she had been waiting to do all day, Pokuwaa arose to watch the coffin lifted onto the shoulders of bearers.

The procession started, and with it, Pokuwaa's real weeping began. No other woman in the procession wept more bitterly. Now her tongue could release itself sufficiently to speak of some of the feelings inside her.

'Oh, Boakye! You have died a miserable death.

'Sleep well.

'Boakye the daring one whose flesh has had to be shared by vultures and forest creatures.

'Sleep well.

'If you knew this would be your end why didn't you stay at home?

'Oh! Oh! Boakye.'

Pokuwaa's tears flowed on. She became so hysterical that everybody's attention was drawn to her. Realizing this, she blew her nose, wiped her tears with her cloth, and tried to check her weeping.

The procession was getting close to the cemetery when the first two of the coffin bearers came to a halt, complaining that they could not move. The coffin toppled off their heads and was caught and helped up again by the helpers who were walking alongside of it.

The bearers seemed to be held up by a force beyond their control. They could not move. People shouted 'Ei! Ei!' as the coffin tried to wrench itself out of restraining hands. A priest rushed forward and poured libation,

> 'Oh, Odomankoma, Amoakye Baafuo,
> Boakye is due to join you.
> Let him enter.
> Permit his remains to be laid to rest.
> Be gracious. Have sympathy.
> Oh, Apeafo, we appeal to you.'

Having thus appealed to the keeper of the spirit world, they waited for results. Moments passed before the bearers could move again. This was one of the things Pokuwaa found particularly difficult to understand.

When they reached the cemetery dusk had already set in. The women stopped weeping to allow the closing rites to be performed. Bats fluttered in the cool sky, dipping their wings as if they meant it as a gesture of condolence to Yaw Boakye. They reminded Pokuwaa so much of the vultures that she was seized by a fresh attack of hysteria, throwing herself about so violently that again she drew attention to herself. Koramoa took hold of her in order to restrain her. Her sobbing mingled with the loud chirping of crickets.

The three widows of Boakye ran forward, each throwing a pot ahead of her, and saying, 'Here are your pots.'

'They are finishing with him,' whispered Pokuwaa through her sobbing. 'They are telling him that the marriage which he arranged with them on this earth is over.'

'Here are your pots!' said the third widow.

Once the pot was thrown, each widow turned round to run back home without looking behind her.

'They have made their parting,' sobbed Pokuwaa.

After the body had been lowered into the pit, she threw a pebble into the grave hoping that it would indeed help her to part with the painful memories surrounding Yaw Boakye's death.

At home that evening, Kwadwo asked her why she had been so hysterical in the funeral procession. He sounded angry about it. Pokuwaa soon found out why.

'They are wondering in Brenhoma, and I myself am wondering also, what there was between you and Yaw Boakye. Tell me. Was there something between you?'

'No, nothing,' said Pokuwaa quietly.

'Well, you wept as though you were his lover,' Kwadwo

said, watching her face with anxiety. 'Why were you weeping in that way?'

Pokuwaa felt at this moment that she should tell Kwadwo everything she knew. But she held herself in check.

'I don't know why I wept so much,' she said. Then a comment that was so much like the Pokuwaa he liked came to relax Kwadwo. 'I must have been a little drunk,' she said, with something resembling a smile. 'Palm wine was flowing so freely there.'

Kwadwo laughed. 'All of us drank,' he said, 'but it didn't make us weep like that. I never wept once.'

'That is as it should be,' said Pokuwaa. 'You are a man. I am a woman.'

Kwadwo patted her arm fondly, and gave up the argument.

For many weeks, Pokuwaa's daily existence was haunted by this unhappy incident. Aware of her nervousness, Kwadwo accompanied her to her farm, and gave her more of his company.

Perhaps it was also because Brenhoma talked so much of Yaw Boakye that it took Pokuwaa such a long time to free herself from her awful memories. There were all the signs that Boakye's death was another event that would be commemorated in the village each year. People began to swear by Yaw Boakye's death. Girls sang in the Asɔgoro about him, until one particular song became an established item:

'Yaw Boakye Akikodɔɔ  'Yaw Boakye who has completely departed,

75

| Wadi akokoduru akowu | He pursued games of bravery to his death. |
| Wawu Akɔ a momma no ɔnna | If he is dead, let him sleep, |
| Momma ɔnna.' | Let him sleep.' |

# Chapter Eleven

KWADWO's fondness for Pokuwaa was growing deeper. Her charm and the warm sympathy which her heart was capable of expressing in so many special ways for him, drew him closer to her. She took special care about feeding him, and even at times when he was sleeping out with his other wife, she was not unwilling to cook him nice things to eat.

In addition, Pokuwaa was good at conversation. She could talk of little experiences with humour, and report little stories told by her friends so playfully that it was a delight to listen to her.

She teased Kwadwo about his great capacity for sleep. 'You sleep and sleep,' she said. 'Sometimes I feel that my role is to keep guard over you at night.'

One night, when someone knocked on the wall to say that one of Kwadwo's children was ill, she had to shake him violently before he stirred.

'A man shouldn't sleep like this,' she rebuked. 'You must sleep less heavily, if you are going to be of any help in an emergency. If we were still fighting wars, you would easily get yourself captured in your sleep.'

Kwadwo, who felt unable to help himself, usually laughed

these comments off his mind. But one day, he heard a comment from Pokuwaa which disturbed him. He was lying down. She must have presumed that he was asleep. She placed her hand on his arm and said sadly, 'What sort of child will a man who sleeps so much have with me? She will sleep so much that she will grow up lazy and become ...'

'What are you saying?' Kwadwo blurted out.

'Oh, aren't you asleep?' Pokuwaa laughed, but Kwadwo did not believe that she hadn't meant her comment seriously. Still, their intimacy continued to grow.

When the dry winds from the north came to warn of the arrival of Opɛbere, Kwadwo made a special effort to please Pokuwaa by cutting and preparing new ground for a new farm for her.

At the height of the dry season, the women had a hard time collecting water. They had much further to walk. The time that Pokuwaa could spare to keep Kwadwo company on the farm was considerably lessened. Only when evening came could they get a spell of leisurely talk with each other, and this they greatly enjoyed.

On evenings when Pokuwaa prepared spices to mix into shea butter, for rubbing into her skin, Kwadwo lay down contentedly watching her and enjoying the perfume. Once she asked him why he didn't use some of the perfumed shea butter himself if he liked it so much. 'What a suggestion!' he retorted. Do you want your neighbours to call me a woman? It is sufficient for me that one of us should smell nice, and that it should be you. I come into this room sometimes, and feel that all the scented herbs of the forest are here.'

Between the two of them life was smiling. There had been

78

no better time for them to produce a child if one was going to come along. Pokuwaa knew this, but she hid from Kwadwo the melancholy that seized her when she thought about it.

On a morning when the village seemed particularly quiet, Pokuwaa sat with this kind of melancholy in her room, rubbing her limbs more profusely than usual with her scented cream. The Opε wind had become very severe. It was drying up everything and threatening to crack the skin on people's lips and limbs. Pokuwaa's black skin responded well to the shea butter, for it shone beautifully.

She walked out into the sun outside. 'What is there to do today?' she asked herself, for she was fighting with the sad thoughts that had continued to rise inside her since Kwadwo left that morning. She picked up a pot to go and get water. The long walk would do her good. The Ananse stream was the only one left with any water in it, and it was a good distance away.

As she walked through the village a woman stopped in the middle of throwing dirty water away and gaped at her. Pokuwaa greeted her absent-mindedly and walked on. The path to the Ananse stream used to run close to the cemetery, but, because reports of seeing ghosts on it had made the people uneasy, they had worked together to clear a new path in the dry season two years ago. Since then, however, the cemetery had edged closer to the new path, because so many people had died.

Walking over small knolls in the path, Pokuwaa came to a fallen log which she climbed. The cemetery was on the other side of this. She could see mounds heaped here and there among the little bushes. She quickly turned her eyes away but she had noticed that the mound closest to her was that of a small child. There was a cooking pot on it, and at the head, a nyamedua with an offering pot nestling in the hollow of its three branches.

'Poor thing,' she said, 'your mother still thinks of you.' As she walked on, she tried to put herself in that mother's place. She would take the same care with the burial of a child. 'Is it any advantage to bear a child only to see it die?' But perhaps the fact of being able to say that you gave birth to a child was the important thing. Why have the pain of the birth and the pain of the loss? Well, the gods knew better. Perhaps if the child lived it would bring unforeseen misery to its parents.

Suddenly the stream was before her. She walked to a small dip between two large stones where the water was held up. Nobody seemed to have come to the stream. The water was full. Little spills flowed over the stones.

Just as she prepared to fill her pot she heard the fluttering of wings and the sharp cry of a bird in pain.

'Hei! Mind! I am here,' she called, thinking that a trapper was in hiding somewhere to hunt birds coming to drink at the stream.

More fluttering of wings, and an eagle flew very low past her. Only a quick movement of her head saved her from getting her face slapped by its powerful wings. A hornbill fell from the branches fluttering its wings in the last pains of dying.

'Well, there are some compensations,' she said. She held the bird down and twisted its neck, took some canna leaves to wrap it, and tore off a creeper to bind it up. Then she filled her pot.

As she stooped down to lift it up to her head, she saw her reflection in the water, and hesitated. Straightening up, she looked at her breasts which were now flat on her chest. She had often noticed this change in her breasts when holding them up as she ran about in the house. But, at this moment, she was reminded that she was ageing. She looked into the water again. Two veins on her chest, running across each other, also told her that she was losing weight and flesh. She sighed heavily, raised her pot onto her head and began her lonely walk back home, carrying the hornbill in her hands. She climbed the knolls and the fallen tree, shifting her head from side to side to organise her balance. When she reached the cemetery she wouldn't look at the graves again. From there, she spent the rest of the time diverting herself. She thought of the neck movements of the priests at times of possession. She thought of the number of times she had carried a yam tuber like a child on her back, occasionally pushing it up to settle it properly, and tightening it more securely with a twist of the ends of her cloth. It didn't seem to have taken her very long to return to the village. As she passed through, many women stared at her without saying anything. She entered her house and put her pot down.

'Look, mother,' she said, 'I came upon an eagle killing a hornbill, and I have brought the hornbill.'

'Where?' her mother asked with fear.

'At the Ananse stream.'

Her mother's mouth fell open. 'But Pokuwaa,' she screamed, 'you knew that today is Akwasidae, on which

81

nobody has any right to go to the Ananse stream. And now, you have not only gone there, but taken the food of the gods as well.'

Pokuwaa stood there amazed, with the hornbill in her hand. When she could speak, she said, 'But who knows that the eagle is the spirit of the stream?'

'Take this thing back,' said her mother, turning away. 'It is only because the times have changed that you have got back without that eagle doing you any harm.'

Pokuwaa felt disturbed now, remembering how the eagle had barely missed slapping her with its wings. She now understood why there had been nobody else at the stream. She had not forgotten that it was Sunday; but that it was also Akwasidae had completely escaped her.

Leaving the house, she passed through the village once more, choosing another route. A few yards into the bush, she threw the hornbill away, and lingered for a while.

'Mother, I have returned the bird,' she said, when she got back home.

'Did you see the eagle again?'

'No.'

'I have a fear. You must purify yourself. It is too big a risk not to do so,' the old lady firmly announced, picking up a yam and making ready to peel it. 'When you want the gods to help you, you do not go wronging them.'

Pokuwaa didn't want to protest. Her mother had come to an age when she brooded endlessly over things she had been quite prepared to ignore in the past. It seemed as if she would keep on talking throughout her preparations for this rite that she was bent on performing. 'We people of Brenhoma believe that anything that happens to a human being connects with that person's soul. We are bound to keep the soul free from evil.'

A feeling Pokuwaa had not experienced before, suddenly came into her. She plugged her fingers into her ears as if she didn't want to hear any more of her mother's talk. Flopping down at the door of her room, she began rubbing her stomach as if the pain of childbirth was upon her. 'I swear by my soul that this is the end for me,' she muttered.

'God help me,' cried her mother, 'what's happening to you, my daughter? Are you in pain, or what?'

'Why are you asking me such questions?' asked Pokuwaa aggressively.

'I have been watching you,' said the old lady, quivering. 'You don't behave normally. I must tell your uncle Kwaku Tawia.'

'There is nothing wrong with me,' said Pokuwaa.

'Well, don't sit on the ground like that.'

Quickly, the old lady mashed the yams which she had boiled with succulent adwera herbs, put the mixture in a calabash, placed six boiled eggs round it and set it before a high white stool.

'Sit here,' she said.

Without a word, Pokuwaa sat on the stool.

'Repeat after me.' Pokuwaa listened carefully and obeyed.

> 'Kra Adwoa, my soul
> Feed on this purifying food.
> You saw this day's encounter,
> Good soul of mine

You deserve the purifying egg,
Come and feed.'

Sighing with relief, the old lady said, 'Thanks to Nyankopɔn. Now eat up the food, Pokuwaa, and don't leave a
single bit.'

With no appetite to help her, it took Pokuwaa a long time
to eat up the whole calabash full of mashed yam, and the
six eggs. Having achieved it, she wanted to get up and
be gone, but her mother wouldn't let her.

'Sit down, there is more left to do,' she ordered.

With a sigh, Pokuwaa shifted a little on her seat, and
waited. Her mother brought out white threads of newly
spun cotton into which a cowrie and other small shells had
been knotted. She tied this round Pokuwaa's left wrist, and
dabbed her face with white clay.

Not wanting to attract attention and invite questions,
Pokuwaa remained in the house for the rest of the day.

Towards evening Koramoa came to visit her. She tried to
tell her about the feeling that had risen inside her that day,
but she did not know how to express it.

'Pokuwaa, I don't want to bruise your wound, but if it is
about the child, you know that my sympathies are with you,'
Koramoa said gently after a long pause in which neither of
them had been able to look at the other's face.

'Koramoa, in all Brenhoma, you are the woman most
intimately associated with me and with the longing of my
life. Hold my hand, and help me to get this statement I have
to make out of my stomach.'

Affectionately, Koramoa circled her with her arm.

84

'I think I am going to have peace at last,' said Pokuwaa. 'I am going to give up crying inside me for that which I cannot get. I am not going to sacrifice any more.'

Koramoa felt unable to say anything. She looked at Pokuwaa expecting to see tears, but she saw that she was calm.

D

# Chapter Twelve

It was dark when Pokuwaa and Koramoa left the house. Under the cloth that covered her shoulders Pokuwaa carried the pot of herbs which she had been using for her washing rites. So that none should suspect what their mission was, they passed through the village in a leisurely strolling manner, as though they were merely taking the night air.

When they finally left the village behind them, Koramoa waited, while her friend went a little way into the bush.

Pokuwaa removed the pot of herbs from under her cloth, held it high, and hurled it away from her. It crashed, breaking into little pieces. She said nothing, for there was nothing more that she wanted to say. The only thought that came to her at that moment was that the act she had just gone through was very much like the act that Yaw Boakye's widows had performed at his burial.

Kwadwo was sitting beside a fire in the yard when she returned home. She joined him there, and because she had nothing to say, she began poking the glowing logs with a stick. Red sparks flew all around.

'What are you trying to do?' asked Kwadwo. 'Burn me?'

Pokuwaa smiled. 'If I burn you, won't I be the one to weep?'

'Where have you been?' he asked.

Trying to make up her mind whether to face Kwadwo now with her decision or not, Pokuwaa did not answer immediately.

'Aren't you going to eat?' she asked, and without waiting for an answer, went into the kitchen, and brought him food.

By the time he had finished eating, Pokuwaa was ready to give him her news.

'Kwadwo,' she said, 'I will not carry out any more sacrifices.'

'Why?' he asked, stopping in the middle of washing his hands.

'I will not go on with the sacrifices. I have given them up.'

Her voice and manner conveyed her seriousness so clearly that Kwadwo began to feel ill at ease.

'But Pokuwaa,' he said, 'how can you say this; unless you mean that you no longer want a child?'

'I am a woman,' said Pokuwaa. 'And a woman does want a child; that is her nature. But if a child will not come, what can I do? I can't spend my whole life bathing in herbs.'

Silence fell between them. In Kwadwo's mind a fear raged that what this further meant was the end of their marriage. She had probably told her mother, who would not hesitate to urge her to divorce him. He felt violent beating in his heart and little flutterings in his stomach.

'Do try to take your mind off such idle thoughts tonight,' he counselled. 'Let us continue to pray. It isn't only for a child that we are praying to the gods. When we go before them, they can see all the other things against which we need their protection. To give up sacrifices is to give up life itself.'

'I am not asking you to agree with my decision,' Poku-waa replied. 'What I want my own self to understand is that there is a force that knows what is good for me.'

Going into her room Pokuwaa took off her cloth and slipped out of the talisman she had been wearing round her waist. A priestess in the next village had given it to her. She opened her brass bowl and took out another talisman. She brought the two into the yard, threw them into the fire, and sat down to watch them flare up and burn.

When she stirred again, the fire was dying down. Inside her, she felt quite calm.

'Kwadwo, come, let us sleep,' she said. It was the longest sleep she had been granted for a very long time. With its refreshment and her new-found calm she was ready to face her mother about noon the following day.

It was Friday. Her mother was ready to attend the weekly drumming session in the house of the fetish Kukuo. She noticed that Pokuwaa was without the purification clay marks.

'Why, Adwoa?' she asked. 'Have you forgotten? How can you forget the very thing you live for?'

'Sit down, mother, and let us talk,' she said. They sat down.

'What is it?' asked the old lady.

'I have stopped the sacrifices. Never again will I perform them. I am taking my mind off the fruitless efforts for a child.'

'Supposing the gods hearing you, decide to take vengeance on you, Adwoa Pokuwaa? Shut up!' Her mother's voice shook. Picking up her stick, she said, 'I know who is responsible for this. It is your husband. He fears that you will divorce him, and he has used charms to take your mind off the very thing you live for. I will consult the medicine man and get an antidote.' She walked out of the house, still talking.

First she went to see the head of the Asona Clan, Opanin Kofi Owusu, to report what Pokuwaa had said.

'If she is not going to do what is necessary, then I must take it out of my mind that I have a daughter. She is like any boy in Brenhoma, for there is no difference between a barren woman and a man.'

'Don't worry,' said Opanin Owusu. 'She will return to reason soon.'

'She ought to,' cried the old woman. 'What is the fate of a state destined to be if its women refuse to give birth? Where are the sons who will defend the land going to come from? A woman who says, "I will not give birth," is useless. Useless!' Sobs choked her. 'I feared there would be no grandchildren to mourn me when I die. In Pokuwaa's decision that fear has become true.'

Opanin Owusu tried to console her as he walked out with her to set her on the path to the fetish house.

# Chapter Thirteen

THE mild rains, which came after Opɛbere had tired out the forest and people with its harsh winds and dryness, seemed to have fallen on Adwoa Pokuwaa herself especially. She filled her days untiringly with long periods of work on the new farm that Kwadwo Fordwuo had cleared for her, always returning home with bounce in her walk and a cheerfulness that began to surprise people.

It was true that having experienced the bad failure of crops during the past year, the people of Brenhoma were paying determined attention to their farms. They had made sure of getting their seed in with the first spell of planting rains, and they now applied themselves to the weeding and staking and fencing that would aid the farms to thrive. A general cheerfulness was abroad in the playful calls that rang in the forest to link friend with friend while they worked. It was because Pokuwaa's vitality was exceptional that people took notice of it.

As the months passed by, Kwadwo's fears that Pokuwaa would leave him melted away in the warmth of her brightness of spirit. It pleased him to hear his friends joking about his capacity to give spirit to his wife. The day he reported this to Pokuwaa, she nearly knocked him down as she protested by playfully struggling with him. He had come with a gift that he had hidden in the kitchen.

'I've been hunting,' he said, when Pokuwaa let go of him.

'For what?' she asked pertly. 'For rats or for the things men hunt?'

'Say Ayekoo to me, Adwoa Pokuwaa,' he rebuked.

'Very well, Ayekoo,' she said, playfully.

'It is in the kitchen,' he said.

She ran out quickly there, and was soon calling out, 'Hei, hei, Kwadwo Fordwuo, today you've brought me a whole antelope? Hei, I have a husband who has treated me like a new bride today. What spirit entered you to make you do it?'

'Are you happy?' asked Kwadwo with smiles.

'Oh, yes, but I hope nobody saw you bringing it. They will begin to whisper that I have spoiled your head completely with charms.'

'All right, that is women's chatter,' said Kwadwo. 'But you deserve it for making my men friends praise me.'

Pokuwaa put her tongue out at him and said, 'Yoo, I have warned you.'

As Kwadwo watched her, he was half-praying, 'May the subject of the child never arise again to depress her spirit.'

Although he was more sure than ever now that Pokuwaa loved him well, the thought of that night, when she made her decision, kept sending out a thorn to prick him from time to time.

Relations with her mother had been difficult for a while after that. Perhaps his occasional anxiety was due to the fact that he still feared her influence on Pokuwaa. He knew that the old lady continued to carry sacrifices of eggs to Tano every Fofie, and that she participated in the weekly drumming sessions at the house of the fetish Kukuo. From these visits she would come back to the house to narrate how she had prayed to the messengers of Onyankopɔn Twedeampong to put her daughter's senses back into her head.

But then, when he considered Pokuwaa herself, her lack of tension, and the way in which she would listen to these reports of her mother's without being in any way disturbed, it sufficed to dismiss his anxiety.

As a matter of fact, the old lady's rage against himself, and her tussle with Pokuwaa, seemed to have abated after a very tough three weeks or so during which there had not been much peace in the house. But that was well over five months behind them. It seemed that all of them had come to an understanding and acceptance of the situation. Quite often these days, the old lady's sympathy for her daughter showed itself in small acts of affectionate help. Pokuwaa would return from the farm in the evenings to find that the pots she had had no time to clean had been washed, and neatly stacked upside down. Ripe plantain, which was a great favourite of hers, would be roasting on the fire, and her mother would be husking roasted groundnuts to go with it, her fingers trembling, but working carefully to keep the nuts unsplit.

Pokuwaa responded well to these considerate acts, and was far more willing to sit and talk with her. There was much that she learned from their long talks after they had eaten their meals in the evenings. Only when Kwadwo came would she rise to attend him. Perhaps it was because age was really claiming the old lady now, and bending her mind more to the spirit world, that she spoke so often and so convincingly of the importance of the soul's harmony in the beliefs of the people of Brenhoma.

Many times, when Kwadwo joined them for these talks, they sat until the night dew dampened their clothes and made them aware of the passing of the night.

The old lady would rise then, saying, 'These old bones must be taken inside and sheltered from the dew. Sleep well, my children.'

After she had retired one night, saying that she didn't want to permit her old bones to kill her before her time with rheumatism, Kwadwo asked Pokuwaa, 'Do you know how old your mother is?' Pokuwaa couldn't say. They found themselves involved in a long discussion of events on which the calculation of their own ages could be based. For no reason that Kwadwo could see, Pokuwaa withdrew into herself suddenly in the middle of this discussion. When he became aware that he had been talking for a while without her seeming to hear him, he took her by her arm and called, 'Pokuwaa, why is your mind so far away?'

She shivered, and all she said was, 'Let's go in. It is cold.' But she knew that she had been trying to make up her mind to tell him, after three months of keeping it to herself, that for three successive months she had not seen a flowing of her blood.

When it happened the first time, she thought about it for a few days, and then she calmly reasoned that it was normal for a woman advancing in years. For fear of stirring up the topic of her barrenness, which she had fought so hard to lay at rest, she counselled herself against reporting the news to her mother. As for Kwadwo himself, why should he know? Their life was happy enough. She permitted the sign to enable her to tie up her resolution in a knot of finality.

After the second month, however, she noticed that her breasts were heavier. The nuts inside them felt as if they were swelling, and they hurt when she squeezed them. This drove her to speculation on the possibility of pregnancy, and threw her mind into great confusion. She found herself often taking her clothes off to stand looking at the shadow her figure cast on the wall of her room, to discover if there was any change in her. She was aware that this was growing into an irresistible habit in spite of her efforts to prevent it from becoming so.

Now the third month had passed. The signs in her breasts were still there. In addition, within the past two weeks, she had noticed a darkening of her navel which had set her heart beating against her will with a hope that she dared not accept but which had begun to fire her blood.

All this was in her mind when she fell silent tonight, and when she went in with Kwadwo, he had no sooner dropped off to sleep than she arose from his side, to turn up the lamp and look at herself. As she did so, a strange conviction took hold of her. She felt that she wanted to dare to hope that it was pregnancy that was causing the signs that had been confusing her. She shivered with the intense excitement she felt, and crept back to Kwadwo to cling to him.

She didn't sleep. Before dawn she was up again. A new

vigour filled her body. Before Kwadwo awoke she had set a fire crackling in the kitchen and placed a large pot of water on it.

Kwadwo was turning sleepily in bed when she returned to him. 'Wake up, Kwadwo,' she said. 'You are going to have your bath in my house today.'

It was an unusual invitation which made Kwadwo sit up immediately.

'What was that you said?' he asked, rubbing his eyes.

'I wanted to be the one to prepare your bath today,' she said tenderly. 'The water is warm. Come.'

All that Kwadwo said was, 'Oh Pokuwaa!' but she knew that he was very pleased.

It was well past sunrise before he left her house. The old lady, sitting in the sun to warm herself, looked up with surprise at them as they came out into the yard together. Pokuwaa took him to the gate and said, 'On your way, please let Koramoa know that I would like to see her this morning.'

Pokuwaa took her bath, and made some cocoyam porridge for herself and her mother. Before they had finished eating, she heard Koramoa's voice as she approached the house telling her son, 'Go back home. Go back home before I smack your buttocks for you.'

'Let him come, Koramoa,' Pokuwaa called out, as she ran to meet her.

'No, let him return,' said Koramoa. 'I've told him to go back, and he must learn to obey. He follows me about as though I were his wife.' She picked up a straw which could not possibly have hurt any child at all, and looked threateningly at her son, who immediately turned about and ran giggling back home.

'The little rascal,' she said, laughing herself. 'Pokuwaa, I greet you. Kwadwo says you want me.'

'That is right, my friend, but don't come in. I will fetch my water pot.'

She fetched it, and said, 'Koramoa, we are going to the Ananse stream.'

'But why do we have to go so far for water at this time of the year?' asked Koramoa.

'That should tell you that there is a special reason,' said Pokuwaa. 'What is the value of a friend? Isn't it true that one ought to be able to say, "Come, my friend, I need you," and be sure that she will come, even if she doesn't know what the reason is?'

'It is true,' said Koramoa. 'Let us go.'

'The pot is not really necessary,' Pokuwaa confided. 'We need it for passing through the village.'

Dismissing curiosity, Koramoa chatted with her friend until they reached the last knoll on the path to the Ananse stream.

'Sit here and wait for me,' said Pokuwaa. 'When we return home, I may have some news to tell you. It may make you sad, or it may make you laugh with me.'

Koramoa was really curious now, but she sat down, and watched her friend descending the knoll, to take a bend in the path and disappear. When Pokuwaa reached the stream, she drew close to the place where the water had collected in the hollow of the two large stones. With her heart beating she set down her pot and bared her breasts. She bent forward and saw her breasts pointing at her, with dark shiny circles above the nipples. A dark line reached from her darkened navel downwards. 'O Twedeampong,' she said, her eyes filling with tears. 'Since I am not sick, these cannot be a sign of disease. I am pregnant. O Twedeampong, I am pregnant.' She threw herself down and sobbed, but she was happy. She gathered her breasts up in her arms like a child, and continued to cry.

When she could stop the tears, she picked up her pot and filled it. Then she scooped up water with her hands to wash her face, lifted her pot to her head, and took the path back, humming a song, and stepping rhythmically to its beat.

Koramoa arose to meet her, and fell into step behind her still wondering, but asking no questions. She caught the song which was a common love song in Brenhoma, and they both sang it, doing a double clapping to mark its pauses.

In this manner, they passed the cemetery without noticing it, and had just entered the village, when some children playing near a pile of firewood shouted, 'Yee!' and pointed cheerfully at Pokuwaa's pot.

'What is the matter?' she asked.

A little girl said, 'Mother, there is a bird on your pot.'

As her arm shot up, she heard a whirr of wings above her head. She and Koramoa both turned to watch the bird flying away towards the forest.

'It was drinking your water from your pot,' said one little girl.

'Quiet,' she said. 'Birds don't drink from pots on people's heads.'

'We saw it,' two or three voices shouted together.

'All right, quiet,' said Pokuwaa, resuming her walk.

After a little silence, Koramoa said, 'Do you know the song about that?'

'About what?' asked Pokuwaa, her heart beating wildly.

'About little birds perching on people's pots to drink?' And she began to sing. Pokuwaa joined in the song. They entered her house still singing it.

'What do you make of this?' shouted Pokuwaa to her mother. 'A bird was drinking from my water pot!'

The old lady had just been dozing in the sun. She rubbed her face and said, 'I don't know, but it ought to be a good sign. We have a song about it.'

'We are singing it,' Koramoa said, and started it again.

Pokuwaa's mother laughed. She arose from her seat. 'Stop,' she said. She hitched her cloth round her middle. 'In our day we sang it with real spirit this way.' She burst out singing. Her stick crashed from her grasp as she started to clap.

'Anoma gye nsu nom . . .'

'Yee! Mother!' Koramoa cried, hopping with amusement, for the old lady could sing it with spirit all right.

> 'Bird, take of my water and drink,
> Drink till you are full,
> Then do not sleep or wander far,
> For when you are full
> There is a task I have to set you,
> The task of watching over my lover.'

Pokuwaa and Koramoa joined in. When she finished singing the old lady picked up her stick and said, 'That is a song from a tale but it is based on a true human story, of course, just like all Anansesɛm.'

'I am glad it happened to me,' said Pokuwaa, her hands raised to her pot to set it down.

'If it means anything, it means that it brings you love,' said her mother.

While Pokuwaa was setting her pot down, her cloth came loose and fell away. Her mother, who was watching her, caught her breath at the sight of her breasts and exclaimed, 'Adwoa! Let me see. Let me see something.' She seized her daughter's breasts in her trembling hands.

'What's this?' she exclaimed. 'Do you feel pain in them? Are they swollen?'

'Hei! She is pregnant,' Koramoa exclaimed. 'Pokuwaa!'

'Let me see,' her mother said again, examining her breasts with her fingers.

'My daughter,' she said, peering into Pokuwaa's watering eyes. 'Great Tano! Is this the situation? Have you become a woman?' She trembled so much that Pokuwaa thought she would fall, and took hold of her to steady her. Picking up her cloth, she went to sit outside her door, followed by the old lady and Koramoa.

'Well, can't you talk?' asked the old lady, still trembling on her stick in front of her.

'Is this what you had to tell me?' asked Koramoa. 'Is this the news? Pokuwaa? Oh! Thanks to Nyankopɔn. Thanks to the Great Benevolent One.'

'Thanks indeed to Nyankopɔn,' Pokuwaa whispered with quivering lips. 'I do believe that I am pregnant.'

'But when, Adwoa? When, Ahwenee?' asked the old lady.

99

'Talk, my child. Do you mean to say that we have been together in this house and you have known you have seed, after
all these years of our sorrowing together, and have not told
me? What have I done to you that you should treat me so?'

'Shall I go, so that you can tell her?' asked Koramoa.

'No, sit down, my sister, for you are not a stranger,' said
Pokuwaa. 'Sit down, mother. Get her a seat for me,
Koramoa.'

When they both sat down, she said, 'I have not seen my
blood for more than three months now.'

'But you didn't tell me?'

'I did not associate it with anything like this. I thought
that all it meant was that I was getting old.'

'Foolishness,' said the old lady. 'What made you think so?
A woman gets well past fifty before her blood stops flowing.
How old are you that you should have such thoughts—you,
who haven't had to spend up your store in uncontrolled
childbearing like the rest of us?'

Before Pokuwaa could prevent her, the old lady was on
her knees, bowing towards the ground and repeating, 'Tano,
you are great indeed. You have not permitted me to carry
my sorrow to the grave. Pokuwaa my child is a woman,
before my eyes. Her womb shelters a baby of bone, flesh and
blood, when I had ceased to hope, and was preparing for
death without having seen a grandchild crawl in this yard.'

She tried to get up, but she couldn't. Pokuwaa helped her
up, saying, 'Mother, Tano has had nothing to do with it. I
know that it is Nyankopɔn Twedeampong who has shown
me this mercy.'

'We sacrificed to Tano,' said her mother sternly.

'But I didn't have to do the bathing or any of the other rites to make this come to me,' Pokuwaa said, pointing to her belly.

Ignoring her protestation, the old lady followed her into her room with a stream of advice. 'Now, you must not do any strenuous work. You have been working too hard. Kwadwo Fordwuo must help you just as your father helped me when I was carrying you in my womb.'

'Kwadwo has not been doing badly at all,' said Pokuwaa.

'You speak the truth, but now that you have this child inside you, he must not permit you to move at all. It is by the mercy of the powerful ones alone that you didn't lose your good fortune with all the hard work you have insisted on doing. Have you told Kwadwo Fordwuo?'

'No,' said Pokuwaa.

'Do you say no? Adwoa Pokuwaa, do you mean that you have not told the man with whom you sleep at night, anything about a thing like this? You are a problem! That is all I can say!'

'Mother, I told you I didn't know. How was I to hope? Supposing I had told you and raised your hopes only to have you suffer disappointment!'

'We will tell Kwadwo Fordwuo now,' said her mother. 'Koramoa, call Kwadwo Fordwuo. Tell him to come to this house now, now, now. Tell him to run.'

'I will,' said Koramoa. 'Adwoa, health to your head. I go to eat an egg on your behalf. And from now on, don't go for water. I will fetch it for you. It is the least I can do to help you to guard your gift to a safe delivery.'

'Thank you,' said Pokuwaa.

# Chapter Fourteen

WHEN Kwadwo Fordwuo was given the news, he couldn't speak. He gazed at Pokuwaa, and at the old lady, as if he suspected some kind of connivance between them.

'Your wife Pokuwaa is pregnant,' repeated the old lady. 'Can't you hear?'

He still didn't respond.

'I am going to find a white chicken to sacrifice for her on Friday,' said the old lady. 'I leave her in your hands.'

After she had left the room, Kwadwo arose from the bed, drew Pokuwaa close to him, and asked, 'Pokuwaa, are we in for trouble again?'

Pokuwaa smiled and said, 'Look for yourself.'

He took off her cloth himself and gazed at her figure in astonishment. Muttering inaudibly, he staggered back to the bed and sat on it, still gazing at her. Presently he said, 'Cover yourself, beautiful one.' While Pokuwaa was doing so, she heard him sobbing. She had never seen Kwadwo's tears. She rushed to sit beside him on the bed where he was crying like a little boy.

'How old is it?' he asked when he stopped.

'I think three months.'

'Is that what you think?'

'That is what I think,' she said.

'It is usual for the woman to tell her husband.'

'I know. It is also not a bad thing for a woman to be afraid of raising the hopes of her husband, when it is important to avoid disappointment.'

Kwadwo fell silent again, but he drew her closer to him and touched her belly. When he spoke, he said, 'We must take a sacrifice of thanksgiving to Tano.'

'I leave that to you,' said Pokuwaa. 'As for me, I am sure that this child does not come from there.'

'I implore you, don't say things like that, Pokuwaa,' said Kwadwo with visible concern.

'Don't let us talk about that then,' said Pokuwaa. 'I have begun saying to Nyankopɔn the thanks which I will continue to say for the rest of my life. His name is Daasebre indeed.'

They spent the rest of the day together, discussing their joy, and all that had led to it.

Pokuwaa's first appearance in Brenhoma, after the news had passed by way of the house of the Asona Clan to break and scatter into every household, proved to be quite an event. People greeted her as though they had never had occasion to do so before. The men congratulated her outright for her good fortune, some saying they would betroth her child to their sons if it was born a girl. 'A girl born by Adwoa Pokuwaa herself should be beautiful,' they said.

Maame Fosua, a fat woman who was well liked for her candid tongue, called her into her house and said, 'My daughter, you have triumphed. The gods never fail to compensate those who have suffered. I am coming to your house to bring you some oranges.' Pokuwaa liked her warmth. She thanked her politely.

'Eat a lot of palm soup,' she said. 'And chew sugar-cane from time to time. Then you won't have trouble with making milk in your breasts.'

Pokuwaa thanked her again.

There were other woman who approached the subject in a more circuitous manner. Particularly one, whom Pokuwaa knew to be the friend of Kwadwo's other wife.

'I hear you haven't been well,' she said.

'I am well enough,' said Pokuwaa.

'Farm work, with all the bending and hoisting that it involves, is hard for us women,' the woman continued. 'Take care of yourself.'

'Thank you,' said Pokuwaa. 'I will take care of myself.'

'You were born a hard-working person,' said the woman, not giving up. 'You are not one of those women who use pregnancy as an excuse for not working. So you will continue to work, I know. But you are sensible. You don't need me to advise you not to work harder than your strength will permit you. How is Kwadwo?'

'He is well enough, thank God,' said Pokuwaa as she broke away.

The woman turned immediately to a mother who was listening through her kitchen window while she fed her breast to her baby.

'The gossip has started,' thought Pokuwaa, when she saw them getting together. She was right.

'She didn't say,' said the woman, 'but I looked at her brow

with an experienced eye. She is pale, and her pulse is beating in that rapid manner just here below her throat.'

'Is that right? She is lucky,' said the mother, snatching her breast from her baby's mouth, and seating him on the window-sill. 'It is so rare for a woman to start childbearing at her age. She must thank the gods properly for their gift, and thank Kwadwo Fordwuo also, who has proved his claim of being a giver of children.'

'Let her lay herself down in complete humility to him,' said the woman. 'Adwoa Pokuwaa is not so humble. But I am probably wasting my breath, because Kwadwo Fordwuo himself permits her to do what she pleases with him.'

'So I hear,' said the mother. The child started to yell and kick, because of the gusts of smoke that had started passing out from the window, so they left the discussion there, and parted.

Under the village silk cotton tree, many calabashes of palm wine passed round amidst male jokes aimed at the man who was expecting a child with such unrivalled pride. If the heavy rains had not let themselves down, and broken up the daily party, the men would have been pleased to continue using Kwadwo to justify long drinking bouts.

Pokuwaa welcomed the wet season, for she could spend time that she needed to spend to prepare her home, in her own house-proud way, for the event that would come after the harvest and after the Odwira.

Red earth must be fetched, for her room was going to have a new floor, and it would have to be polished every week until it showed a high glossy surface. She could not sew garments for the baby, because she shared the belief that it was presumptuous to do so before it had been born. But Kwadwo had brought her three of his old cloths. She would tear them up into lengths, wash, fold and pack them carefully in one of her brass bowls. They would be enough to keep her baby clean.

There were spices to grind, mix and shape into small oval rolls, and then dried to a hardness that would permit them to be rubbed on a stone without crumbling. There were plantain stems to be beaten into soft fibre and arranged into circular pads for drying the baby, and soap to be made from dried plantain skins, ashes and herbs.

The rain could not dampen her spirits. Her mother, Koramoa and Kwadwo were around her; her child inside her, kicking.

Kwadwo Fordwuo! He came through the downpour. He brought out a bundle tied in a piece of white cloth, and said, 'Untie it, Pokuwaa.' She unwrapped a beautiful Kente cloth.

'I will not wait for the day of our child's naming ceremony to bring you gifts,' he said, smiling. 'Take it, it is yours.'

Pokuwaa picked up the lamp and went close to him where he was standing drying himself. She lifted the lamp to his face and asked, 'Kwadwo, what are you going to call our child?'

'Isn't that to be revealed at the naming ceremony?'

'Well, by this gift you have already anticipated the day,' she said.

Kwadwo laughed. 'It is going to be a girl,' he said. 'It is going to be a girl, and she will be called Adwoa.'

'Don't say Adwoa Pokuwaa,' she laughed.

'No, not Pokuwaa, for there should be only one Pokuwaa amongst us. I will name her Adwoa Menenkyem.'

'Oh, Kwadwo, can't we call her Adwoa Nyamekyɛ?'

Kwadwo looked at her, his eyes full of laughter. 'Do you really believe I haven't thought of that?'

'And if it is a boy?' asked Pokuwaa. 'If it is a boy?'

He saw that she was smiling brightly at him, and that her eyes were the eyes of a woman who loved him.

'You talk too much, Adwoa Pokuwaa,' he said.

# Glossary

| | |
|---|---|
| *fetish child* | a child born through the help of a god or goddess |
| *madwowa* | the ovary |
| *Yaa Peafo* | response to greetings |
| *okra* | the soul |
| *akyikyibaso* | the equivalent of an engagement ring, it is made of red parrot's feathers and a couple of cowries, and is worn on the wrist of a young woman about to be married |
| *kra Adwoa* | *kra*—soul; *Adwoa*—name of a female child born on a Monday |
| *Ama Foriwa* | *Ama*—child born on a Saturday; *Foriwa*—family name from Ofori |
| *kente* | a locally woven cloth of colourful design worn on festive occasions |
| *Nyamekye* | 'the gift of God the Almighty' (*Nyame*—God; *kye*—gift) |